BORDER, BREED
NOR BIRTH

MORE WILDSIDE CLASSICS

Please see www.wildsidepress.com for a complete list!

BORDER, BREED NOR BIRTH

MACK REYNOLDS

WILDSIDE PRESS

BORDER, BREED NOR BIRTH

Originally published as a 2-part serial in *Analog* magazine, July-August 1962 issues.

This edition published in 2009 by Wildside Press, LLC.
www.wildsidebooks.com

I

El Hassan, would-be tyrant of all North Africa, was on the run.

His followers at this point numbered six, one of whom was a wisp of a twenty-four year old girl. Arrayed against him and his dream, he knew, was the combined power of the world in the form of the Reunited Nations, and, in addition, such individual powers as the United States of the Americas, the Soviet Complex, Common Europe, the French Community, the British Commonwealth and the Arab Union, working both together and unilaterally.

Immediate survival depended upon getting into the Great Erg of the Sahara where even the greatest powers the world had ever developed would have their work cut out locating El Hassan and his people.

Bey-ag-Akhamouk who was riding next to Elmer Allen in the lead air cushion hover-lorry, held a hand high. Both of the solar powered desert vehicles ground to a halt.

Homer Crawford vaulted out of the seat of the second lorry before it had settled to the sand. "What's up, Bey?" he called.

Bey pointed to the south and west. They were in the vicinity of Tessalit, in what was once known as French Sudan, and immediately to the south of Algeria. They were deliberately avoiding what little existed in this area in the way of trails, the Tanezrouft route which crossed the Sahara from Colomb-Béchar to Gao, on the Niger, was some fifty miles to the west.

Homer Crawford stared up into the sky in the direction Bey pointed and his face went wan.

The others were piling out of the vehicles.

"What is it?" Isobel Cunningham said, squinting and trying to catch what the others had already spotted.

"Aircraft," Bey growled. "A rocket-plane."

"Which means the military in this part of the world," Homer said.

The rest of them looked to him for instructions, but Bey suddenly took over. He said to Homer, "You better get on over beneath that outcropping of rock. The rest of us will handle this."

Homer looked at him.

Bey said, flatly, "If one of the rest of us gets it, or even if all of us do, the El Hassan movement goes on. But if something happens to you, the movement dies. We've already taken our stand

and too much is at stake to risk your life."

Homer Crawford opened his mouth to protest, then closed it. He reached inside the solar-powered lorry and fetched forth a Tommy-Noiseless and started for the rock outcropping at a trot. Having made his decision, he wasn't going to cramp Bey-ag-Akhamouk's style with needless palaver.

Isobel Cunningham, Cliff Jackson, Elmer Allen and Kenny Ballalou gathered around the tall, American educated Tuareg.

"What's the plan?" Elmer said. Either he or Kenny Ballalou could have taken over as competently, but they were as capable of taking orders as giving them, a desirable trait in fighting men.

Bey was still staring at the oncoming speck. He growled, "We can't even hope he hasn't seen the pillars of sand and dust these vehicles throw up. He's spotted us all right. And we've got to figure he's looking for us, even though we can hope he's not."

The side of his mouth began to tic, characteristically. "He'll make three passes. The first one high, as an initial check. The second time he'll come in low just to make sure. The third pass and he'll clobber us."

The aircraft was coming on, high but nearer now.

"So," Elmer said reasonably, "we either get him the second pass he makes, or we've had it." The young Jamaican's lips were thinned back over his excellent teeth, as always when he went into combat.

"That's it," Bey agreed. "Kenny, you and Cliff get the flac rifle, and have it handy in the back of the second truck. Be sure he doesn't see it on this first pass. Elmer, get on the radio and check anything he sends."

Kenny Ballalou and the hulking Cliff Jackson ran to carry out orders.

Isobel said, "Got an extra gun for me?"

Bey scowled at her. "You better get over there with Homer where it's safer."

She said evenly, "I've always considered myself a pacifist, but when somebody starts shooting at me, I forget about it and am inclined to shoot back."

"I haven't got time to argue with you," Bey said. "There aren't any extra guns except handguns and they'd be useless." As he spoke, he pulled his own Tommy-Noiseless from its scabbard on the front door of the air cushion lorry, and checked its clip of two hundred .10 caliber ultra-high velocity rounds. He flicked the selector to the explosive side of the clip.

The plane was roaring in on what would be its first pass, if Bey had guessed correctly. If he had guessed incorrectly, this might be the end. A charge of neopalm would fry everything for a quarter of a mile around, or the craft might even be equipped with a mini-fission bomb. In this area a minor nuclear explosion would probably go undetected.

Bey yelled, "Don't anybody even try to fire at him at this range. He'll be back. It takes half the sky to turn around in with that crate, but he'll be back, lower next time."

Cliff Jackson said cheerlessly, "Maybe he's just looking for us. He won't necessarily take a crack at us."

Bey grunted. "Elmer?"

"Nothing on the radio," Elmer said. "If he was just scouting us out, he'd report to his base. But if his orders are to clobber us, then he wouldn't put it on the air."

The plane was turning in the sky, coming back.

Cliff argued, "Well, we can't fire unless we know if he's just hunting us out, or trying to do us in."

Elmer said patiently, "For just finding us, that first pass would be all he needed. He could radio back that he'd found us. But if he comes in again, he's looking for trouble."

"Here he comes!" Bey yelled. "Kenny-Cliff . . . the rifle!"

Isobel suddenly dashed out into the sands a dozen yards or so from the vehicles and began running around and around in a circle as though demented.

Bey stared at her. "Get back here," he roared. "Under one of the trucks!"

She ignored him.

The rocketplane was coming in, low and obviously as slow as the pilot could retard its speed.

The flac rifle began jumping and tracers reached out from it—inaccurately. The Tommy-Noiseless automatics in the hands of Bey and Elmer Allen gave their silenced flic flic flic sounds, equally ineffective.

On the ultra-stubby wings of the fast moving aircraft, a row of brilliant cherries flickered and a row of explosive shells plowed across the desert, digging twin ditches, miraculously going between the air cushion lorries but missing both. It was upon them, over and gone, before the men on the ground could turn to fire after.

Elmer Allen muttered an obscenity under his breath.

Cliff Jackson looked around in desperation. "What can we do now? He won't come close enough for us to even fire at him, next time."

Bey said nothing. Isobel had collapsed into the sand. Elmer Allen looked over at her. "Nice try, Isobel," he said. "I think he came in lower and slower than he would have otherwise—trying to see what the devil it was you were doing."

She shrugged, hopelessly.

"Hey!" Kenny Ballalou pointed.

The rocketcraft was wobbling, shuddering, in the sky. Suddenly it burst into a black cloud of fire and smoke and explosion.

At the same moment, Homer Crawford got up from the sand dune behind which he'd stationed himself and plowed awkwardly through the sand toward them.

Bey glared at him.

Homer shrugged and said, "I checked the way he came in the first time and figured he'd repeat the run. Then I got behind that dune there and faced in the other direction and started firing where I thought he'd be, a few seconds before he came over. He evidently ran right into it."

Bey said indignantly, "Look, wise guy, you're no longer the leader of a five-man Reunited Nations African Development Project team. Then, you were expendable. Now, you're El Hassan. You give the orders. Other people are expendable."

Homer Crawford grinned at him, somewhat ruefully and held up his hands as though in supplication. "Listen to the man, is that any way to talk to El Hassan?"

Elmer Allen said worriedly, "He's right, though, Homer. You shouldn't take chances."

Homer Crawford went serious. "Actually, none of us should, if we can avoid it. In a way, El Hassan isn't one person. It's this team here, and Jake Armstrong, who by this time I hope is on his way to the States."

Bey was shaking his head in stubborn determination. "No," he said. "I'm not sure that you comprehend this yourself, Homer, but you're Number One. You're the symbol, the hero these people are going to follow if we put this thing over. They couldn't understand a sextet leadership. They want a leader, someone to dominate and tell them what to do. A team you need, admittedly, but not so much as the team needs you. Remember Alexander? He had a team starting off with Aristotle for a brain-trust, and Parmenion, one of the greatest generals of all time for his right-hand man. Then he had a group of field men such as Ptolemy, Antipater, Antigonus and Seleucus—not to be rivaled until Napoleon built his team, two thousand years later. And what happened to this super-team when Alexander died?"

Homer looked at him thoughtfully.

Bey wound it up doggedly. "You're our Alexander. Our Caesar. Our Napoleon. So don't go getting yourself killed, damn it. Excuse me, Isobel."

Isobel grinned her pixielike grin. "I agree," she said. "Damn it."

Homer said, "I'm not sure I go all along with you or not. We'll think about it." His voice took a sharper note. "Let's go over and see if there's enough left in that wreckage to give us an idea of who the pilot represented. I can't believe it was a Reunited Nations man, and I'd like to know who, of our potential enemies, dislikes the idea of El Hassan so much that they figure we should all be bumped off before we even get under way."

It had begun—if there is ever a beginning—in Dakar. In the offices of Sven Zetterberg the Swedish head of the Sahara Division of the African Development Project of the Reunited Nations.

Homer Crawford, head of a five-man trouble-shooting team, had reported for orders. In one hand he held them, when he was ushered into the other's presence.

Zetterberg shook hands abruptly, said, "Sit down, Dr. Crawford."

Homer Crawford looked at the secretary who had ushered him in.

Zetterberg said, scowling, "What's the matter?"

"I think I have something to be discussed privately."

The secretary shrugged and turned and left.

Zetterberg, still scowling, resumed his own place behind the desk and said, "Claud Hansen is a trusted Reunited Nations man. What could possibly be so secret . . . ?"

Homer indicated the orders he held. "This assignment. It takes some consideration."

Sven Zetterberg was not a patient man. He said, in irritation, "It should be perfectly clear. This El Hassan we've been hearing so much about. This mystery man come out of the desert attempting to unify all North America. We want to talk to him."

"Why?" Crawford said.

"Confound it," Zetterberg snapped. "I thought we'd gone into this yesterday. In spite of the complaints that come into this office in regard to your cavalier tactics in carrying out your assignments, you and your team are our most competent operatives. So we've given you the assignment of finding El Hassan."

"I mean, why do you want to talk to him?"

The Swede glared at him for a moment, as though the American was being deliberately dense. "Dr. Crawford," he said, "when the African Development Project was first begun we had high hopes. Seemingly all Reunited Nations members were being motivated by high humanitarian reasons. Our task was to bring all Africa to a level of progress comparable to the advanced nations. It was more than a duty, it was a crying need, a demand. Africa is and has been throughout history a have-not continent. While Europe, the Americas, Australia and now even Asia, industrialized and largely conquered man's old socio-economic problems, Africa lagged behind. The reasons were manifold, colonialism, lingering tribal society . . . various others. Now that very lagging has become a potential explosive situation. With the coming of antibiotics and other break-throughs in medicine, the African population is growing with an all but geometric progression. So fast is it growing, that what advances were being made did less than keep up the level of per capita gross product. It was bad enough to have a per capita gross product averaging less than a hundred dollars a year, but it actually sank below that point."

Homer Crawford was nodding.

Zetterberg continued the basic lecture with which he knew the other was already completely familiar. "So the Reunited Nations took on the task of advancing as rapidly as possible the African economy and all the things that must be done before an economy can be advanced. It was self-preservation, I suppose. Have-not nations, not to speak of have-not races and have-not continents, have a tendency eventually to explode upon their wealthier neighbors."

The Swede pressed his lips together before continuing.

"Unfortunately, the Reunited Nations as the United Nations and the League of Nations before it, is composed of members each with its own irons in the fire. Each with its own plans and schemes." His voice was bitter now. "The Arab Union with its desire to unite all Islam into one. The Soviet Complex with its ultimate dream of a soviet world. The capitalistic economies of the British Commonwealth, Common Europe, and your United States of the Americas, with their hunger for, positive need for, sources of raw materials and markets for their manufactured products. All, though playing lip service to the African Development Project, have still their own ambitions."

Sven Zetterberg waggled a finger at Homer Crawford. "I do not charge that your United States is attempting to take over Africa, or even any section of it, in the old colonialistic sense. Even England and France have discovered that it is much simpler to dominate economically than to go through all the expense and effort of governing another people. That is the basic reason they gave up their empires. No, your United States would love to so dominate Africa that her products, her entrepreneurs, would flood the continent to the virtual exclusion of such economic competitors as Common Europe. The Commonwealth feels the same, so does the French Community. The Soviets and Arabs have different motivations, but they, too, wish to take over. The result . . ." The Swede tossed up his hands in a gesture more Gallic than Scandinavian.

"What has all this got to do with El Hassan?" Homer Crawford asked softly.

The Swede leaned forward. "If we more devoted adherents of the Reunited Nations are ever to see our hopes come true, Africa must be united and made strong. And this must be done through the efforts of Africans not Russians, British, French, Arabs . . . nor even Scandinavians. Socio-economic changes should not, possibly cannot, be inflicted upon a people from without. Look at the mess the Russians made in such countries as Hungary, or the Americans in such as South Korea."

"The people themselves must have the dream," Crawford said softly.

"I beg your pardon?"

"Nothing. Go on."

Zetterberg said, "On the surface, great progress seems to be continuing. Afforestation of the Sahara, the solar pumps creating new oases, the water purification plants on the Atlantic and Mediterranean, pushing back the desert, the oil fields, the mines, the roads, the damming of the Niger. But already cracks can be seen. A week or so ago, a team of Cubans, supposedly, at least, in the Sudan to improve sugar refining methods, were machine-gunned to death. By whom? By the Sudanese? Unlikely. No, this Cuban massacre was one of many recent signs of conflict between the great powers in their efforts to dominate. Our problem, of course, deals only with North Africa, but I have heard rumors in Geneva that much the same situation is developing in the south as well.

"At any rate, Dr. Crawford, when the rumors of El Hassan began to come into this office they brought with them a breath of hope. From all we have heard, he teaches our basic program—a breaking down of old tribal society, education, economic progress, Pan-African unity. Dr. Crawford, no one with whom this office is connected seems ever to have seen this El Hassan but we are most anxious to talk to him. Perhaps this is the man behind whom we can throw our support. Your task is to find him."

Homer Crawford raked the fingers of his right hand back over his short wiry hair, and grimaced. He said, "It won't be necessary."

"I beg your pardon, Doctor?"

Crawford said, "It won't be necessary to go looking for El Hassan."

The Swede scowled his irritation at the other. "See here . . ."

Crawford said, "I'm El Hassan."

Sven Zetterberg stared at him, uncomprehending.

Homer Crawford said, "I suppose it's your turn to listen and for me to do the talking." He shifted in his chair, uncomfortably. "Dr. Zetterberg, even before the Reunited Nations evolved the idea of the African Development Project, it became obvious that the field work was going to have to be in the hands of Negroes. The reason is doublefold. First, the African doesn't trust the white man, for good reason. Second, the white man is a citizen of his own country, first of all, and finds it difficult not to have motives connected with his own race and nation. But the African Negro, too, has his tribal and sometimes national affiliations and cannot be trusted not to be prejudiced in their favor. The answer? The educated American Negro, such as myself.

"I haven't the slightest idea from whence came my ancestors, from what part of Africa, what tribe, what nation. But I am a Negro and . . . well, have the dream of bettering my race. I have no irons in the fire, beyond altruistic ones. Of course, when I say American Negroes I don't exclude Canadian ones, or those of Latin America or the Caribbean. It is simply that there are greater numbers of educated American Negroes than you find elsewhere."

Zetterberg said impatiently, "Please, Dr. Crawford. Come to the point. That ridiculous statement you made about El Hassan."

"Of course, I am merely giving background. Most of we field workers, not only the African Development teams, but such organizations as the Africa for Africans Association and the representatives of the African Department of the British Commonwealth, and of the French Community's African Affairs sector, are composed of Negroes."

Zetterberg was nodding. "All right, I know."

Homer Crawford said, "The teams of all these organizations do their best to spur African progress, in our case, in North Africa, especially the area between the Niger and the Mediterranean. Often we disguise ourselves as natives since in that manner we are more quickly trusted. We wear the clothes, speak the local language or lingua franca."

The American hesitated a moment, then plunged in. "Dr. Zetterberg, the African is still a primitive but newly beginning to move out of a tradition-ritual-taboo tribal society. He seeks a hero to follow, a man of towering prestige who knows the answers to all questions. We may not like this fact, we with our traditions of democracy, but it is so. The African is simply not yet at that stage of society where political democracy is applicable."

"My team does most of its work posing as Enaden—low caste itinerant smiths of the Sahara. As such we can go any place and are everywhere accepted, a necessary sector of the Saharan economy. As such, we continually spread the . . . ah, propaganda of the Reunited Nations—the need for education, the need for taking jobs on the new projects, the need for casting aside old institutions and embracing the new. Early in the game we found our words had little weight coming from simple Enaden smiths so we . . . well, invented this mysterious El Hassan, and everything we said we attributed to him.

"News spreads fast in the desert, astonishingly fast. El Hassan started with us but soon other teams, hearing about him and realizing that his message was the same as that they were trying to propagate, did the same thing. That is, attributed the messages they had to spread to El Hassan. It was amusing when a group of us got together last week in Timbuktu, to find that we'd all taken to kowtowing to this mythical desert hero who planned to unite all North Africa."

The Swede was staring at him unbelievingly. "But, a bit earlier you said you were El Hassan."

Homer Crawford looked into his chief's face and nodded seriously. "I've been conferring with various other field workers, both Reunited Nations and otherwise. The situation calls for a real El Hassan. If we don't provide him, someone else will. I propose to take over the position."

Sven Zetterberg's face was suddenly cold. "And why, Dr. Crawford, do you think you are more qualified than others?"

The American Negro could hardly fail to note the other's disapproval. He said evenly, but definitely, "Through experience. Through education. Through . . . through having the dream, Dr. Zetterberg."

"The Reunited Nations cannot support such a project, Dr. Crawford. I absolutely forbid you to consider it."

"Forbid me?"

It was as though a strange something entered the atmosphere of the room, almost as though a new presence was there. And almost, it seemed to Sven Zetterberg, that the already tall, solidly built man across from him grew physically as his voice seemed to swell, to reach out, to dominate. There was a new, and all but unbelievable Homer Crawford here.

The Swedish official regathered his forces. This was ridiculous. He said again, "I forbid you to . . ." the sentence dribbled away under the cold disdain in the air now.

Homer Crawford said flatly, "You don't seem to understand, Zetterberg. The Reunited Nations has no control over El Hassan. Homer Crawford, as of this meeting, has resigned his post with the African Development Project. And El Hassan has begun his task of uniting all North Africa."

Sven Zetterberg, shaken by this new and unsuspected force the other seemed to be able to bring to his command, fought back.

"It will be simple to discredit you, to let it be known that you are no more than an ambitious American out to seize power illegally."

Crawford's scorn held an element of amusement. "Try it. I suspect your attempts to discredit El Hassan will prove unsuccessful. He has already been rumored to be everything from an Ethiopian to the Second Coming of the Messiah. Your attempt to brand him an American adventurer will be swallowed up in the flood of other rumor."

The Swede was still shaken by the strange manner in which his once subordinate had suddenly dominated him. Sven Zetterberg was not a man to be dominated, to be made unsure.

Time folded back on itself and for a moment he was again a lad and on vacation with his father in Bavaria. They were having lunch in the famed Hofbraühaus, largest of the Munich beercellars, and even a ten-year-old could sense an anticipation in the air, particularly among the large number of brownshirted men who had gathered to one side of the ground level of the beer hall. His father was telling Sven of the history of the medieval building when a silence fell. Into the beerhall had come a pasty faced, trenchcoat garbed little man, his face set in stern lines but insufficiently to offset the ludicrous mustache. He was accompanied by an elderly soldier in the uniform of a Field Marshal, by a large tub of a man whose face beamed—but evilly—and by a pinch faced cripple. All were men of command, all except the pasty faced one, to whom they seemingly and surprisingly, deferred. And then he stood on a heavy chair and spoke. And then his power reached out and grasped all within reach of his shrill voice. Grasped them and compelled them and they became a shouting, red faced, arm brandishing mob, demanding to be led to glory. And Sven's father had bustled the shocked boy from the building.

It came back to him now, clearly and forcefully, and he realized that whatever it was with which the Beast of Berchtesgaden had enchanted his people, that power was on call in Homer Crawford. Whether he used it for good or evil, that enchanting power was on call. And again Sven Zetterberg was shaken.

Homer Crawford was on his feet, preparatory to leaving.

The Swede simply had to reassert himself. "Dr. Crawford, the Reunited Nations is not without resources. You'll be arrested before you leave Dakar."

An element of the tenseness left the air when Crawford smiled and said, "Doctor, for several years now I have been playing hide and seek in the Sahara, doing your work. You mentioned earlier that my team is the most experienced and capable. Just whom are you going to send to pick me up? Members of some of the other teams? Old friends and comrades in arms. Many of whom owe their lives to my team when all bets were down. Please do send them, Doctor, I am going to need recruits."

He swung and left the office and even as he went could hear the angry Reunited Nations chief blasting into an interoffice communicator. He decided he'd better see if there wasn't a back door or window through which to leave the building. He'd have to phone Bey, Isobel and the others and get together for a meeting to plan developments. El Hassan was getting off to a fast start, already he was on the lam.

Homer Crawford played it safe. From the nearest public phone he called Isobel Cunningham at the Hotel Juan-le-Pin. No matter how fast Sven Zetterberg swung into action, it would take his operatives some time to connect Isobel with Homer and his team. As an employee of the Africa for Africans Association, she would ordinarily come in little contact with the Reunited Nations teams.

He said, "Isobel? Homer here. Can you talk?"

She said, "Cliff and Jake are here."

He said, "Have you sounded them out? How do they feel about the El Hassan project?"

"They're in. At least, Jake is. We're still arguing with Cliff."

"O.K. Now listen, carefully. Zetterberg turned thumbs down on the whole deal, for various reasons we can discuss later. In fact, he's incensed and threatened to take steps to keep us from leaving Dakar."

Isobel was alerted but she snorted deprecation. "What do you want?"

"They're probably already looking for me, and in a matter of minutes will probably try to pick up Bey-ag-Akhamouk, Elmer Allen and Kenny Ballalou, the other members of my team. Get in touch with them immediately and tell them to get into native costume and into hiding. You and Jake—and Cliff—do the same."

"Right. Where do we meet and when?"

"In the souk, in the food market. There's a native restaurant there, run by a former Vietnamese. We'll meet there at approximately noon."

"Right. Anything else?"

Homer said, "Tell Bey to bring along an extra 9mm Recoilless for me."

"Yes, El Hassan," she said, her voice expressionless. She didn't waste time. Homer Crawford heard the phone click as she hung up.

He was in a branch building of the post and telegraph network on the Rue des Resistance. Before leaving it, he looked out a window. Half a block away was the office of the Sahara Division of the African Development Project. Even as he watched, a dozen men hurried out the front door, fanned out in all directions.

Homer grinned sourly. Old Sven was moving fast.

He shot a quick glance around the lobby of the building. He had to get going. Zetterberg had started with a dozen men to trail down El Hassan. He'd probably have a hundred involved before the hour was out.

A corridor turned off to the right. Homer hurried down it. At each door he looked inside. To whoever occupied the room he murmured a few words of apology in Wolof, the Sengalese lingua franca. The fourth office was empty.

Homer stood there before it for a long, agonizing moment, waiting for the right person to pass. Finally, the man he needed came along. About six feet tall, about a hundred and eighty; dressed in the local native dress and on the ragged side.

Homer said to him authoritatively, in the Wolof tongue, "You there, come in here!" He opened the door, and pointed into the office.

The other, taken aback, demurred.

Homer's face and tone went still more commanding. "Step in here, before I call the police."

It was all a mistake, of course. The Senegalese made the gesture equivalent to the European's shrug, and entered the office.

Homer came in behind him, closed the door. He wasted no time in preliminaries. Before the native turned, the American's hand lashed out in a karate blow which stunned the other. Homer Crawford caught him, even as he fell, and lowered him gently to the floor.

"Sorry, old boy," he muttered, "but this is probably the most profitable thing that's happened to you this year."

He stripped off the other's clothes; as rapidly as he could make his hands fly. The other was still out and probably would be for another ten minutes, Crawford estimated. He stripped off his own clothes and donned the native's.

Last of all, he took his wallet from his pocket, divided the money it contained and stuffed a considerable wad of it into the European clothing he was abandoning.

"Don't spend all of that in one place," he growled softly.

Homer dragged the other to a side of the room so that the body could not be spotted from the entrance. Then he crossed to the door, opened it and stepped into the corridor beyond.

There was no need for sulking. He walked out the front door and headed away from the dock and administration buildings area and toward the native section, passing the Reunited Nations building on the way.

Dakar teems with multitudes of a dozen tribes come in from the jungles and the bush, the desert and the swamp areas of the sources of the Niger, to look for work on the new projects, to visit relatives, to market for the products of civilization—or to gawk. Homer Crawford disappeared into them. One among many.

Toward noon, he entered the cleared area which was the restaurant he had named to Isobel and squatted before the pots to the far end of the Vietnamese owned eatery, examining them with care. He chose a large chunk of barbequed goat and was served it with a half pound piece of unsalted Senegalese bread, torn from a monstrous loaf, and a twisted piece of newspaper into which had been measured an ounce or so of coarse salt. He took his meal and went to as secluded a corner as he could find.

Homer Crawford chuckled inwardly. That morning he had breakfasted in the most swank hotel in West Africa. He wished there was some manner in which he could have invited Sven Zetterberg to dine here with him. Or, come to think of it, a group of the students he had once taught sociology at the University of Michigan. Or, possibly, prexy Wallington, under whom he had worked while taking his doctor's degree.

Yes, it would have been interesting to have had a luncheon companion.

A native woman, on the stoutish side but with her hair done up in one of the fabulously ornate hair styles specialized in by the Senegalese, and wearing a flowing, shapeless dress of the garish textiles run off purposely for this market in Japan and Manchester, waddled up to take a place nearby. She bore a huge skewar of barbequed beef chunks, and a hunk of bread not unlike Homer's own.

She grumbled uncomfortably, her back to the American, as she settled into a position on the floor. And she mumbled as she began chewing at the meat.

No table manners, Homer Crawford grinned inwardly. He wondered how long it would take for the others to get here. He wasn't worried about Isobel, Cliff Jackson and Jake Armstrong. It would take time before Zetterberg's Reunited Nations cloak and dagger boys got around to them, but he wasn't sure that she'd be able to locate his own team in time. That bit he'd given the Swede official about his being so bully-bully with the other Reunited Nations teams was in the way of being an exaggeration, with the idea of throwing the other off. Actually, working in the field on definite assignments, it was seldom you ran into other African Development Project men. But perhaps it would tie Zetterberg up, wondering just who he could trust to send looking for El Hassan.

He finished off his barbequed goat and the bread and wiped his hands on his clothes. Nobody here yet. To have an excuse for staying, he would have to buy a bottle of Gazelle beer, the cheap Senegalese brew which came in quart bottles and was warm and on the gassy side.

It was then that the woman in front of him, without turning, said softly, "El Hassan?"

II

Homer Crawford stared at her, unbelievingly. The woman couldn't possibly be an emmissary from Isobel or from one of his own companions. This situation demanded the utmost secrecy, they hadn't had time to screen any outsiders as to trustworthiness.

She turned. It was Isobel. She chuckled softly, "You should see your face."

His eyes went to her figure.

"Done with mirrors," Isobel said. "Or, at least, with pillows."

Homer didn't waste time. "Where are the others? They should be here by now."

"We figured that the fewer of us seen on the streets, the better. So they're waiting for you. Since I was the most easily disguised, the least suspicious looking, I was elected to come get you."

"Waiting where?"

She licked the side of her mouth, a disconcerting characteristic of hers, and looked at him archly. "Those pals of yours have quite a bit on the ball on their own. They decided that there was a fairly good chance that Sven Zetterberg wasn't exactly going to fall into your arms, so they took preliminary measures. Kenny Ballalou rented a small house, here in the native quarter. We've all rendezvoused there. See, you aren't the only one on the ball."

Homer frowned at her, for the moment being in no mood for humor. "What was the idea of sitting here for the past five minutes without even speaking? You must have recognized me, knowing what to look for."

She nodded. "I . . . I wasn't sure, Homer, but I had the darnedest feeling I was being followed."

His glance was sharp now. First at her, then a quick darting around the vicinity. "Woman's intuition," he snapped, "or something substantial?"

She frowned at him. "I'm not a ninny, Homer."

His voice softened and he said quickly, "Don't misunderstand, Isobel. I know that."

She forgot about her objection to his tone. "Even intuition doesn't come out of a clear sky. Something sparks it. Subconscious psi, possibly, but a spark."

"However?" he prodded.

"I took all precautions. I can't seem to put my finger on anything."

"O.K.," he said decisively. "Let's go then." He came to his feet and reached a hand down for her.

"Heavens to Betsy," she said, "don't do that."

"What?"

"Help a woman in public. You'll look suspicious." She came to her own feet, without aid.

Damn, he thought. She was right. The last thing he wanted was to draw attention to a man who acted peculiarly.

They made their way out of the food market and into the souk proper, Homer walking three or four paces ahead of her, Isobel demurely behind, her eyes on the ground. They passed the native stands and tiny shops, and the even smaller venders and hucksters with their products of the mass production industries of East and West, side by side with the native handicrafts ranging from carved wooden statues, jewelry, gris gris charms and kambu fetishes, to ceramics whose designs went back to an age before the Portuguese first cruised off this coast. And everywhere was color; there are no people on earth more color conscious than the Senegalese.

Isobel guided him, her voice quiet and still maintaining its uncharacteristic demure quality.

He would never have recognized Isobel, Homer Crawford told himself. Isobel Cunningham, late of Columbia University where she'd taken her Master's in anthropology. Isobel Cunningham, whom he had told on their first meeting that she looked like the former singing star, Lena Horne. Isobel Cunningham, slight of build, pixie of face, crisply modern American with her tongue and wit. Was he in love with her? He didn't know. El Hassan had no time, at present, for those things love implied.

She said, "Here," and led the way down a brick paved passage to a small house, almost a hut, that lay beyond.

Homer Crawford looked about him critically before entering. He said, "I suppose this has been scouted out adequately. Where's the back entrance?" He scowled. "Haven't the boys posted a sentry?"

A voice next to his ear said pleasantly, "Stick 'em up, stranger. Where'd you get that zoot suit?"

He jerked his head about. There was a very small opening in the wooden wall next to him. It was Kenny Ballalou's voice.

"Zoot suit, yet!" Homer snorted. "I haven't heard that term

since I was in rompers."

"You in rompers I'd like to see," Kenny snorted in his turn. "Come on in, everybody's here."

The aged, unpainted, warped, wooden house consisted of two rooms, the one three times as large as the second. The furniture was minimal, but there was sitting room on chair, stool and bed for the seven of them.

"Hail, O El Hassan!" Elmer Allen called sourly, as Homer entered.

"And the hail with you," Homer called back, then, "Oops, sorry, Isobel."

Isobel put her hands on her hips, greatly widened by the stuffing she'd placed beneath her skirts. "Look," she said. "Thus far, the El Hassan organization, which claims rule of all North Africa, consists of six men and one dame . . . ah, that is, one lady. Just so the lady won't continually feel that she's being a drag on the conversation, you are hearby allowed in moments of stress such shocking profanity as an occasional damn or hell. But only if said lady is also allowed such expletives during periods of similar stress."

Everyone laughed, and found chairs.

"I'm in love with Isobel Cunningham," Bey announced definitely.

"Second the motion," Elmer said.

The rest of them called, "Aye."

"O.K.," Homer Crawford said glumly, "I can see that this is going to be one tight knit organization. Six men in love with the one dame . . . ah, that is, lady. Kind of a reverse harem deal. Oh, this is going to lead to great co-operation."

They laughed again and then Jake said, "Well, what's the story, Homer? How does the El Hassan project sound to Zetterberg and the Reunited Nations?"

Cliff Jackson laughed bitterly. "Why do you think we're in hiding?" Only he and Jake Armstrong wore western clothing. Kenny Ballalou, Bey-ag-Akhamouk and Elmer Allen were in native dress, similar to that of Homer Crawford. Elmer Allen even bore a pilgrim's staff.

Crawford, glad that the edge of tenseness had been taken off the group by the banter with Isobel, turned serious now.

He said, "This is where we each take our stand. You can turn back at this point, any one of you, and things will undoubtedly go on as before. You'll keep your jobs, have no marks against you. Beyond this point, and there's no turning back. I want you all to think it over, before coming to any snap decisions."

Elmer Allen said, his face wearing its usual all but sullen expression. "How about you?"

Homer said evenly, "I've already taken my stand."

Kenny Ballalou yawned and said, "I've been in this team for three or four years, I'm too lazy to switch now Besides, I've always wanted to be a corrupt politician. Can I be treasurer in this El Hassan regime?"

"No," Homer said. "Bey?"

Bey-ag-Akhamouk said, "I've always wanted to be a general. I'll come in under those circumstances."

Homer said, his voice still even. "That's out. From this point in, you're a Field Marshal and Minister of Defense."

"Shucks," Bey said. "I'd always wanted to be a general."

Homer Crawford said dryly, "Doesn't anybody take this seriously? It's probably going to mean all your necks before it's through, you know."

Elmer Allen said dourly, "I take it seriously. I spent the idealistic years, the school years, working for peace, democracy, a better world. Now, here I am, helping to attempt to establish a tyranny over half the continent of my racial background. But I'm in."

"Right," Homer said, the side of his mouth twitching. "You can be our Minister of Propaganda."

"Minister of Propaganda!" Elmer wailed. "You mean like Goebbels? Me!"

Homer laughed. "O.K., we'll call it Minister of Information, or Press Secretary to El Hassan. It all means the same thing." He looked at Jacob Armstrong and said, "How old are you, Jake?"

"That's none of your business," the white-haired Jake said aggressively. "I'm in. El Hassan is the only answer. North Africa has got to be united, both for internal and external purposes. If you . . . if we . . . don't do the job first, somebody else will, and off hand, I can't think of anybody else I trust. I'm in."

Homer Crawford looked at him for a long moment. "Yes," he said finally. "Of course you are. Jake, you've just been made our combined Foreign Minister and Plenipotentiary Extraordinary to the Reunited Nations. You'll leave immediately, first for Geneva, to present our demands to the Reunited Nations, then to New York."

"What do I do in New York?" Jake Armstrong said blankly, trying to assimilate the curves that were being thrown to him.

"You raise money and support from starry eyed Negro groups and individuals. You line up such organizations as the Africa for Africans Association behind El Hassan. You give speeches, and ruin your liver eating at banquets every night in the week. You send out releases to the press. You get all the publicity for the El Hassan movement you can. You send official protests to the governments of every country in the world, every time they do something that doesn't fit in with our needs. You locate recruits and send them here to Africa to take over some of the load. I don't have to tell you what to do. You can think on your feet as well as I can. Do what is necessary. You're our Foreign Minister. Don't let us see your face again until El Hassan is in control of North Africa."

Jake Armstrong blinked. "How will I prove I'm your representative? I'll need more than just a note To Whom It May Concern."

Homer Crawford thought about that.

Bey said, "One of our first jobs is going to have to be to capture a town where they have a broadcast station, say Zinder or In Salah. When we do, we'll announce that you're Foreign Minister."

Crawford nodded. "That's obviously the ticket. By that time you should be in New York, with an office opened."

Jake rubbed a black hand over his cheek as though checking his morning shave. "It's going to take some money to get started. Once started I can depend on contributions, perhaps, but at first . . ."

Homer interrupted with, "Cliff, you're Minister of the Treasury. Raise some money."

"Eh?" Cliff Jackson said blankly. The king-size, easy-going Californian looked more like the early Joe Louis than ever.

Everybody laughed. Elmer Allen came forth with his wallet and began pulling out such notes as it contained. "I don't know what we'd be doing with this in the desert," he said.

Isobel said, "I have almost three thousand dollars in a checking account in New York. Let's see if I have my checkbook here."

The others were going through their pockets. As bank notes in

British pounds, American dollars, French francs and Common Europe marks emerged they were tossed to the center of the small table which wobbled on three legs in the middle of the room.

Elmer Allen said, "I have an account with the Bank of Jamaica in Kingston. About four hundred pounds, I think. I'll have it transferRed."

Cliff took up the money and began counting it, making notations on a notebook pad as he went.

Bey said, "We're only going to be able to give Jake part of this."

"How's that?" Elmer growled. "What use have we for money in the Sahara? Jake's got to put up a decent front in Geneva and New York."

Bey said doggedly, "As Defense Minister, I'm opposed to El Hassan's followers ever taking anything without generous payment. We'll need food and various services. From the beginning, we're going to have to pay our way. We can't afford to let rumors start going around that we're nothing but a bunch of brigands."

"Bey's right," Homer nodded. "The El Hassan movement is going to have to maintain itself on the highest ethical level. We're going to take over where the French Camel Corps left off and police North Africa. There can't be a man from Somaliland to Mauretania who can say that one of El Hassan's followers liberated him from as much as a date."

Kenny Ballalou said, "You can always requisition whatever you need and give them a receipt, and then we'll pay off when we come to power."

"That's out!" Bey snapped. "Most of these people can't read. And even those that do don't trust what they read. A piece of paper, in their eyes, is no return for some goats, or flour, camels, horses, or whatever else it might be we need. No, we're going to have to pay our way."

Crawford raked a hand back through his wiry hair. "Bey's right, Kenny. It's going to be a rough go, especially at first."

Kenny snorted. "What do you mean, at first? What's going to happen, at second to make it any easier? Where're we going to get all this money we'll need to pay for even what we ourselves use, not to speak of the thousands of men we're going to have to have if El Hassan is ever to come to power?"

Bey's eyebrows went up in shocked innocence. "Kenny, dear boy, don't misunderstand. We don't requisition anything from individuals, or clans, or small settlements. But if we take over a town such as Gao, or Niamey, or Colomb-Béchar, or wherever, there is nothing to say that a legal government such as that of El Hassan, can't requisition the contents of the local banks."

Homer Crawford said with dignity, "The term, my dear Minister of Defense, currently is to nationalize the bank. Whether or not we wish to have the banks remain nationalized, after we take over, we can figure out later. But in the early stages, I'm afraid we're going to have to nationalize just about every bank we come in contact with."

Cliff Jackson said cautiously, "I haven't said whether or not I'll come in yet, but just as a point, I might mention issuing your own legal tender. As soon as you liberate a printing press somewhere, of course."

Everyone was charmed at the idea.

Isobel said, "You can see Cliff was meant to be Minister of Treasury. He's got wholesale larceny in his soul, none of this picayunish stuff such as robbing nomads of their sheep."

Elmer Allen was shaking his head sadly. "This whole conversation started with Bey protesting that we couldn't allow ourselves to be thought of as brigands. Now listen to you all."

Kenny Ballalou said with considerable dignity, "See here, friend. Don't you know the difference between brigandage and international finance?"

"No," Elmer said flatly.

"Hm-m-m," Kenny said.

"Let's get on with this," Homer said. "The forming of El Hassan's basic government is beginning to take on aspects of a minstrel show. Then we've all declared ourselves in . . . except Cliff."

All eyes turned to the bulky Californian.

He sat scowling.

Homer said, easily, "You're not being urged, Cliff. You can turn back at this point."

Elmer Allen growled, "You came to Africa to help your race develop its continent. To conquer such problems as sufficient food, clothing and shelter for all. To bring education and decent medical care to a people who have had possibly the lowest living standards anywhere. Can you see any way of achieving this beyond the El Hassan movement?"

Cliff looked at him, still scowling stubbornly. "That's not why I came to Africa."

Their eyes were all on him, but they remained silent.

He said, defensively, "I'm no do-gooder. I took a job with the Africa for Africans Association because it was the best job I could find."

Isobel broke the silence by saying softly. "I doubt it, Cliff."

The big man stood up from where he'd been seated on the bed. "O.K., O.K. Possibly there were other angles. I wanted to travel. Wanted to see Africa. Besides, it was good background for some future job. I figured it wouldn't hurt me any, in later years, applying for some future job. Maybe with some Negro concern in the States. I'd be able to say I'd put in a few years in Africa. Something like a Jew in New York who was a veteran of the Israel-Arab wars, before the debacle."

They still looked at him, none of them accusingly.

He was irritated as he paced. "Don't you see? Everybody doesn't have this dream that Homer's always talking about. That doesn't mean I'm abnormal. I just don't have the interest you do. All I want is a good job, some money in the bank, security back in the States. I'm not interested in dashing all over the globe, getting shot at, dying for some ideal."

Homer said gently, "It's up to you, Cliff. Nobody's twisting your arm."

There was sweat on the big man's forehead. "All I came to Africa for was the job, the money I got out of it," he repeated, insisting.

To Homer Crawford suddenly came the realization that the other needed an out, an excuse. An explanation to himself for doing something he wanted to do but wouldn't admit because it went against the opportunistic code he told himself he followed.

Homer said, "All right. How much are you making as a field worker for the Africa for Africans Association?"

Cliff looked at him, uncomprehending. "Eight thousand dollars, plus expenses."

"O.K., we'll double that. Sixteen thousand to begin with, as El Hassan's Minister of Treasury and whatever other duties we can think of to hang on you."

There was a long moment of silence, unbroken by any of the others. Finally in a gesture of desperation, Cliff Jackson waved at the money and checks sitting on the center table. "Sixteen thousand a year! The whole organization doesn't have enough to pay me six months' salary."

Homer said mildly, "That's why your pay was doubled. You have to take risks to make money in this world, Cliff. If El Hassan does come to power, undoubtedly you'll get other raises—along with greater responsibility."

He looked into Cliff Jackson's face, and although his words had dealt with money, a man's dream looked out from his eyes. And the force of personality that could emanate from Homer Crawford, possibly unbeknownst to himself, flooded over the huge Californian. The others in the room could feel it. Elmer Allen cleared his throat; Isobel held her elbows to her sides, in a feminine protest against naked male psychic strength.

Kenny Ballalou said without inflection, "Put up or shut up, Cliff old pal."

Cliff Jackson sank back onto the spot on the bed he'd occupied before. "I'm in," he muttered, so softly as hardly to be heard.

"None of you are in," a voice from the doorway said.

The figure that stood there held a thin, but heavy calibered automatic in his hand.

He was a dapper man, neat, trim, smart. His clothes were those of Greater Washington, rather than Dakar and West Africa. His facial expression seemed overly alert, overly bright, and his features were more Caucasian than Negroid.

He said, "I believe you all know me. Fredric Ostrander."

"Of the Central Intelligence Agency," Homer Crawford said dryly. He as well as Bey, Elmer and Kenny had risen to their feet when the newcomer entered from the smaller of the hut's two rooms. "What's the gun for Ostrander?"

"You're under arrest," the C.I.A. man said evenly.

Elmer Allen snorted. "Under whose authority are you working? As a Jamaican, I'm a citizen of the West Indies and a subject of Her Majesty."

"We'll figure that out later," Ostrander rapped. "I'm sure the appropriate Commonwealth authorities will co-operate with the State Department and the Reunited Nations in this matter." The gun unwaveringly went from one of them to the other, retraced itself.

Bey looked at Homer Crawford.

Crawford shook his head gently.

He said to the newcomer, "The question still stands, Ostrander. Under whose authority are you operating? I don't think you have jurisdiction over us. We're in Africa, not in the United States of the Americas."

Ostrander said tightly, "Right now I'm operating under the authority of this weapon in my hand. Dr. Crawford. Do you realize that all of you Americans here are risking your citizenship?"

Kenny Ballalou said, "Oh? Tell us more, Mr. State Department man."

"You're serving in the armed forces of a foreign power."

Even the dour Elmer Allen laughed at that one.

Crawford said, "The fact of the matter is, we are the foreign power."

"You're not amusing, Dr. Crawford," Ostrander said. "I've kept up with this situation since you had that conference in Timbuktu. The State Department has no intention of allowing some opportunist, backed by known communists and fellow travelers, to seize power in this portion of the world. In a matter of months the Soviets would be in here."

Isobel said evenly, "I was formerly a member of the Party. I no longer am. I am an active opponent of the Soviet Complex at the moment, especially in regard to its activity in Africa."

Ostrander snorted his disbelief.

Elmer Allen said, "You chaps never forget, do you?" He looked at the others and explained. "Back during college days, I signed a few peace petitions, that sort of thing. Ever since, every time I come in contact with these people, you'd think I was Lenin or Trotsky."

Homer Crawford said, "My opinion is, Ostrander, that you've had to move too quickly to check back with your superiors. Has the State Department actually instructed you to arrest me and my companions here on foreign soil, without a warrant?"

Ostrander clipped, "That's my responsibility. I'm taking you all in. We'll solve such problems as jurisdiction and warrants when I get you to the Reunited Nations headquarters."

"Ah?" Homer Crawford said. "And then what happens to us?"

Ostrander jiggled the gun, impatiently. "Sven Zetterberg is of the opinion that you should immediately be flown out of Africa and the case brought before the High Council of the African Development Project. What measures will be taken beyond that point I have no way of knowing."

Bey took a step to the left, Kenny Ballalou one to the right. Homer Crawford remained immediately before the C.I.A. operative, his hands slightly out from his sides, palms slightly forward.

Ostrander snapped, "I'm prepared to fire, you men. I don't underestimate the importance of this situation. If your crazy scheme makes any progress at all, it might well result in the death of thousands. I know your background, Crawford. You once taught judo in the Marines. I'm not unfamiliar with the art myself."

Isobel had a hand to her mouth, her eyes were wide. "Boys, don't . . ." she began.

Elmer Allen had been leaning on his pilgrim's staff, as though weary with this whole matter. He said to Ostrander, interestedly, "So you've been checked out on judo? Know anything about the use of the quarterstaff?"

Ostrander kept his gun traversing between, the four of them. "Eh?" he said.

Elmer Allen shifted his grip on his staff infinitesimally. Of a sudden, the end of the staff, now gripped with both hands near the center, moved at invisibly high speed. There was a crack of the wrist bone, and the gun went flying. The other end of the staff flicked out and rapped the C.I.A. operative smartly on the head.

Fredric Ostrander crumbled to the floor.

"Confound it, Elmer," Crawford said. "What'd you have to go and do that for? I wanted to talk to him some more and send a message back to Zetterberg. Sooner or later we've got to make our peace with the Reunited Nations."

Elmer said embarrassedly, "Sorry, it just happened. I was merely going to knock the gun out of his hand, but then I couldn't help myself. I was tired of hearing that holier-than-thou voice of his."

Kenny Ballalou looked down at the fallen man gloomily. "He'll be out for an hour. You're lucky you didn't crack his skull."

"Holy Mackerel," Cliff Jackson said. "I'm going to have to learn to operate one of those things."

Elmer Allen handed him the supposed pilgrim's staff. "Best hand-to-hand combat weapon ever invented," he said. "The British yeoman's quarterstaff. Of course, this is a modernized version. Made of epoxy resin glass-fiber material, treated to look like wood. That stuff can turn a high-velocity bullet, let alone a sword, and it can be bent in a ninety degree arc without the slightest effect, although it'd take a power-driven testing machine to do it."

"All right, all right," Homer said. "We haven't got time for lessons in the use of the quarterstaff. Let's put some thought to this situation. If Ostrander here was able to find us, somebody else would, too."

Isobel licked the side of her mouth. "He was probably following me. Remember, I told you Homer?"

Kenny said, "If he had anyone with him, he'd have brought them along to cover him. You've got to give him credit for bravery, taking on the whole bunch of us by himself."

"Um-m-m," Homer said. "I wish he was with us instead of against us."

Jake Armstrong said, "Well, this solves one problem."

They looked at him.

He said, "Just as sure as sure, he's got a car parked somewhere. A car with some sort of United States or Reunited Nations emblem on it."

"So what?" Kenny said.

"So you've got to get out of town before the search for you really gets under way. With such a car, you can get past any roadblock that might already be up between here and the Yoff airport."

Elmer Allen had sunk to his knees and was searching the fallen C.I.A. man. He came up with car keys and a wallet.

Homer said to Jake Armstrong, "Why the Yoff airport?"

"Our plane is there," Jake told him. "The one assigned Isobel, Cliff and me by the AFAA. You're going to have to make time. Get somewhere out in the ah, boondocks, where you can begin operations."

Bey said thoughtfully, "He's right, Homer. Anybody against us, like our friend here"—he nodded at Ostrander—"is going to try to get us quick, before we can get the El Hassan movement under way. We've got to get out of Dakar and into some area where they'll have their work cut out trying to locate us."

Homer Crawford accepted their council. "O.K., let's get going. Jake, you'll stay in Dakar, and at first play innocent. As soon as possible, take plane for Geneva. As soon as you're there, send out press releases to all the news associations and the larger papers. Announce yourself as Foreign Minister of El Hassan and demand that he be recognized as the legal head of state of all North Africa."

"Wow," Cliff Jackson said.

"Then play it by ear," Homer finished.

He turned to the others. "Bey, where'd you leave our two hover-lorries when you came here to Dakar?"

"Stashed away in the ruins of a former mansion in Timbuktu. Hired two Songhai to watch them."

"O.K. Cliff, you're the only one in European dress. Take this wallet of Ostrander's. You'll drive the car. If we run into any road-blocks between here and the Yoff airport, slow down a little and hold the wallet out to show your supposed identification. They won't take the time to check the photo. Bluff your way past, don't completely stop the car."

"What happens if they do stop us?" Cliff said worriedly.

Kenny Ballalou said, "That'll be just too bad for them."

Bey stooped and scooped up the fallen automatic of Fredric Ostrander and tucked it into the voluminous folds of his native robe. "Here we go again," he said.

III

The man whose undercover name was Anton, landed at Gibraltar in a BEA roco-jet, passed quickly through customs and immigration with his Commonwealth passport and made his way into town. He checked with a Bobby and found that he had a two-hour wait until the Mons Capa ferry left for Tangier, and spent the time wandering up and down Main Street, staring into the Indian shops with their tax-free cameras from Common Europe, textiles from England, optical equipment from Japan, and cheap souvenirs from everywhere. Gibraltar, the tourist's shopping paradise.

The trip between Gibraltar and Tangier takes approximately two hours. If you've never made it before, you stand on deck and watch Spain recede behind you, and Africa loom closer. This was where Hercules supposedly threw up his Pillars, Gibraltar being the one on the European shore. Those who have made the trip again and again, sit down in the bar and enjoy the tax-free prices. The man named Anton stood on the deck. He was African by birth, but he'd never been to Morocco before.

When he landed, he made the initial error of expecting the local citizenry to speak Arabic. They didn't. Rif, a Berber tongue, was the first language. The man called Anton had to speak French to make known his needs. He took a Chico cab up from the port to the El Minza hotel, immediately off the Plaza de France, the main square of the European section.

At the hotel entrance were two jet-black doormen attired in a pseudo-Moroccan costume of red fez, voluminous pants and yellow barusha slippers. They made no note of his complexion, there is no color bar in the Islamic world.

He had reservations at the desk. He left his passport there to go through the standard routine, including being checked by the police, had his bag sent up to his room and, a few minutes later, hands nonchalantly in pockets, strolled along the Rue de Liberté toward the casbah area of the medina. Up from the native section of town streamed hordes of costumed Rifs, Arabs, Berbers of a dozen tribes, even an occasional Blue Man. At least half the women still wore the haik and veil, half the men the burnoose. Africa changes slowly, the man called Anton admitted to himself all over again—so slowly.

Down from the European section, which could have been a

Californian city, filtered every nation of the West, from every section of Common Europe, the Americas, the Soviet Complex. If any city in the world is a melting pot, it is Tangier, where Africa meets Europe and where East meets West.

He passed through the teaming Grand Zocco market, and through the gates of the old city. He took Rue Singhalese, the only street in the medina wide enough to accommodate a vehicle and went almost as far as the Zocco Chico, once considered the most notorious square in the world.

For a moment the man called Anton stood before one of the Indian shops and stared at the window's contents. Carved ivory statuettes from the Far East, cameras from Japan, ebony figurines, chess sets of water jade, gimcracks from everywhere.

A Hindu stood in the doorway and rubbed his hands in a gesture so stereotyped as to be ludicrous. "Sir, would you like to enter my shop? I have amazing bargains."

The man they called Anton entered.

He looked about the shop, otherwise empty of customers. Vaguely, he wondered if the other ever sold anything, and, if so, to whom.

He said, "I was looking for an ivory elephant, from the East."

The Indian's eyebrows rose. "A white elephant?"

"A red elephant," the man called Anton said.

"In here," the Hindu said evenly, and led the way to the rear.

The rooms beyond were comfortable but not ostentatious. They passed through a livingroom-study to an office beyond. The door was open and the Indian merely gestured in the way of introduction, and then left.

Kirill Menzhinsky, agent superior of the Chrezvychainaya Komissiya for North Africa, looked up from his desk, smiled his pleasure, came to his feet and held out his hand.

"Anton!" he said. "I've been expecting you."

The man they called Anton smiled honestly and shook. "Kirill," he said. "It's been a long time."

The other motioned to a comfortable armchair, resumed his own seat. "It's been a long time all right—almost five years. As I recall, I was slung over your shoulder, and you were wading through those confounded swamps. The . . ."

"The Everglades."

"Yes." The heavy-set Russian espionage chief chuckled. "You

are much stronger than you look, Anton. As I recall, I ordered you to abandon me."

The wiry Negro grunted deprecation. "You were delirious from your wound."

The Russian came to his feet, turned his back and went to a small improvised bar. He said, his voice low, "No, Anton, I wasn't delirious. Perhaps a bit afraid, but then the baying of dogs is disconcerting."

The man they called Anton said, "It is all over now."

The Russian returned and said, "A drink, Anton? As I recall you were never the man to refuse a drink. Scotch, bourbon, vodka?"

The other shrugged. "I believe in drinking the local product. What is the beverage of Tangier?"

Kirill Menzhinsky took up a full bottle the contents of which had a greenish, somewhat oily tinge. "Absinthe," he said. "Guaranteed to turn your brains to mush if you take it long enough. What was the name of that French painter . . . ?"

"Toulouse Lautrec," Anton supplied. "I thought the stuff was illegal these days." He watched the other add water to the potent liqueur.

The Russian chuckled. "Nothing is illegal in Tangier, my dear Anton, except the Party." He laughed at his own joke and handed the other his glass. He poured himself a jolt of vodka and returned to his chair. "To the world revolution, Anton."

The Negro saluted with his drink. "The revolution!"

They drank.

The Russian put down his glass and sighed. "I wish we were some place in our own lands, Anton. Dinner, many drinks, perhaps some girls, eh?"

Anton shrugged. "Another time, Kirill."

"Yes. As it is, we should not be seen together. Nor, for that matter should you even return here. The imperialists are not stupid. Very possibly, American and Common Europe espionage agents know of this headquarters. Not to speak of the Arab Union. I shall try to give you the whole story and your assignment in this next half hour. Then you should depart immediately."

The man they called Anton sipped his drink and relaxed in his chair. He looked at his superior without comment.

The Russian took another jolt of his water-clear drink. "Have you ever heard of El Hassan?"

The Negro thought a moment before saying, "Vaguely. Evidently an Arab, or possibly a Tuareg. North African nationalist. No, that wouldn't be the word, since he is international. At any rate, he seems to be drawing a following in the Sahara and as far south as the Sudan. Backs modernization and wants unity of all North Africa. Is he connected with the Party?"

The espionage chief was shaking his head. "That is the answer I expected you to give, and is approximately what anyone else would have said. Actually, there is no such person as El Hassan."

Anton frowned. "I'm afraid you're wrong there, Kirill. I've heard about him in half a dozen places. Very mysterious figure. Nobody seems to have seen him, but word of his program is passed around from Ethiopia to Mauretania."

The Russian was shaking his head negatively. "That I know. It's a rather strange story and one rather hard to believe if it wasn't for the fact that one of my operatives was in on the, ah, manufacturing of this Saharan leader."

"Manufacturing?"

"I'll give you the details later. Were you acquainted with Abraham Baker, the American comrade?"

"Were? I am acquainted with him. Abe is a friend as well as a comrade."

The Russian shook his head again. "Baker is dead, Anton. As you possibly know, his assignment for the past few years has been with a Reunited Nations African Development Project team, working in the Sahara region. We planted him there expecting the time to arrive when his services would be of considerable value. He worked with a five-man team headed by a Dr. Homer Crawford and largely the team's task was to eliminate bottlenecks that developed as the various modernization projects spread over the desert."

"But what's this got to do with manufacturing El Hassan?"

"I'm coming to that. Crawford's team, including Comrade Baker, usually disguised themselves as Enaden smiths. As such, their opinions carried little weight so in order to spread Reunited Nations propaganda, they hit upon the idea of imputing everything they said to this great hero of the desert, El Hassan."

"I see," the man called Anton said.

"Others, without knowing the origin of our El Hassan, took

up the idea and spread it. These nomads are at an ethnic level where they want a hero to follow, a leader. So in order to give prestige to their teachings the various organizations trying to advance North Africa followed in Crawford's footsteps and attributed their teachings to this mysterious El Hassan."

"And it snowballed."

"Correct! But the point is that after a time Crawford came around to the belief that there should be a real El Hassan. That the primary task at this point is to unite the area, to break down the old tribal society and introduce the populace to the new world."

"He's probably right," the man called Anton growled. He finished his drink, got up from his chair and on his own went over and mixed another. "More vodka?" he asked.

"Please." The Russian held up his glass and went on talking. "Yes, undoubtedly that is what is needed at this point. As it is, things are trending toward a collapse. The imperialists, especially the Americans, of course, wish to dominate the area for their capitalistic purposes. The Arab Union wishes to take over in toto and make it part of their Islamic world. We, of course, cannot afford to let either succeed."

The Negro resumed his chair, sipped at his drink and listened, nodding from time to time.

Kirill Menzhinsky said, "As you know, Marx and Engels when founding scientific socialism had no expectation that their followers would first come to power in such backward countries as the Russia of 1917 or the China of 1949. In fact, the establishment of true socialism presupposes a highly developed industrial economy. It is simply impossible without such an economy. When Lenin came to power in 1917, as a result of the chaotic conditions that prevailed upon the military collapse of Imperial Russia, he had no expectation of going it alone, as the British would say. He expected immediate revolutions in such countries as Germany and France and supposed that these more advanced countries would then come to the assistance of the Soviet Union and all would advance together to true socialism."

"It didn't work out that way," the man called Anton said dryly.

"No, it didn't. And Lenin didn't live to see the steps that Stalin would take in order to build the necessary industrial base in Russia." Kirill Menzhinsky looked about the room, almost as though checking to see if anyone else was listening. "Some of our more unorthodox theoreticians are inclined to think that had Lenin survived the assassin's bullet, that Comrade Stalin would have found it necessary to, ah, liquidate him."

The Russian cleared his throat. "Be that as it may, basic changes were made in Marxist teachings to fit into Stalin's and later Khrushchev's new concepts of the worker's State. And the Soviet Union muddled through, as the British have it. Today, the Soviet Complex is as powerful as the imperialist powers."

The espionage leader knocked back his vodka with a practiced stiff wristed motion. "Which brings us to the present and to North Africa." He leaned forward in emphasis. "Comrade, if the past half century and more has taught us anything, it is that you cannot establish socialism in a really backward country. In short, communism is impossible in North Africa at this point in her social evolution. Impossible. You cannot go directly from tribal society to communism. At this historic point, there is no place for the party's program in North Africa."

The man called Anton scowled.

The Russian waggled his hand negatively. "Yes, yes. I know. Ultimately, the whole world must become Soviet. Only that way will we achieve our eventual goal. But that is the long view. Realistically, we must face it, as the Yankees say. This area is not at present soil for our seed."

"Things move fast these days," the Negro growled. "Industrialization, education, can be a geometric progression."

His superior nodded emphatically. "Of course, and as little as ten or fifteen years from now, given progress at the present rate, perhaps there will be opportunity for our movement. But now? No."

The other said, "What has all this to do with El Hassan, or Crawford, or whatever the man's name is?"

"Yes," the Russian said. "Homer Crawford has evidently decided to become El Hassan."

"Ahhh."

"Yes. At this point, in short, he is traveling in our direction. He is doing what we realize must be done."

"Then we will support him?"

"Now we come to the point, Anton. Homer Crawford is not sympathetic to the Party. To the contrary. Our suspicion, although we have no proof, is that he killed Comrade Abe Baker, when

Baker approached him on his stand in regard to the Party's long view."

"I see," the man called Anton said.

The Russian nodded. "We must keep in some sort of touch with him—some sort of control. If this El Hassan realizes his scheme and unites all North Africa, sooner or later we will have to deal with him. If he is antagonistic, we will have to find means to liquidate him."

"And my assignment . . . ?"

"He will be gathering followers at this point. Many followers, most of whom will be unknown to him. You will become one of them. Raise yourself to as high a rank as you find possible in his group. Become a close friend, if that can be done . . ."

"He killed Abe Baker, eh?"

The Russian frowned. "This is an assignment, Comrade Anton. There is no room for personal feelings. You are a good field man. Among the best. You are being given this task because the Party feels you are the man for it. Possibly it is an assignment that will take years in the fulfilling."

The Negro said nothing.

"Are there any questions?"

"Do we have any other operatives working on this?"

The frown became a scowl. "An Isobel Cunningham worked with Comrade Baker, but it has been suspected that she has been drifting away from the party these past few years. Her present status is unknown, but she is believed to be with Homer Crawford and his followers. Possibly she has defected. If so, you will take whatever measures seem necessary. You will be working almost completely on your own, Comrade. You must think on your feet, as the Yankees say."

The man called Anton thought a moment. He said, "You'd better give me as thorough a run down as possible on this Homer Crawford and his immediate followers."

Menzhinsky settled back in his chair and took up a sheaf of papers from the desk. "We have fairly complete dossiers. I'll give you the highlights, then you can take these with you to your hotel to study at leisure."

He took up the first sheet. "Homer Crawford. Born in Detroit of working-class parents. In his late teens interrupted his education to come to Africa where he joined elements of the F.L.N. in

Morocco and took part in several forays into Algeria. Evidently was wounded and invalided back to the States where he resumed his education. When he came of military age, he joined the Marine Corps and spent the usual, ah, hitch I believe they call it. Following that, he resumed his education, finally taking a doctor's degree in sociology. He then taught for a time until the Reunited Nations began its African program. He accepted a position, and soon distinguished himself."

The Russian took up another paper. "According to Comrade Baker's reports, Crawford is an outstanding personality, dominating others, even in spite of himself. He would make a top party man. Idealistic, strong, clever, ruthless when ruthlessness is called for."

Menzhinsky paused for a moment, finding words hard to come by from an ultra-materialist. His tone went wry. "Comrade Baker also reported a somewhat mystical quality in our friend Crawford. An ability in times of emotional crisis to break down men's mental barriers against him. A force that . . ."

The other raised his eyebrows.

His superior chuckled, ruefully. "Comrade Baker was evidently much swayed by the man's personality. However, Anton, I might point out that similar reports have come down to us of such a dominating personality in Lenin, and, to a lesser degree, in Stalin." He twisted his mouth. "History leads us to believe that such personalities as Jesus and Mohammed seemed to have some power beyond that of we more mundane types."

"And the others?" Anton said.

The Russian took up still another paper. "Elmer Allen. Born of small farmer background on the outskirts of Kingston, on the island of Jamaica. Managed to work his way through the University of Kingston where he took a master's degree in sociology. At one time he was thought to be Party material and was active in several organizations that held social connotations, pacifist groups and so forth. However, he was never induced to join the Party. Upon graduation, he immediately took employment with the Reunited Nations and was assigned to Homer Crawford's team. He is evidently in accord with Crawford's aims as El Hassan."

The espionage chief took up another sheet. "Bey-ag-Akhamouk . . ."

The other scowled. "That can't be an American name."

"No. He is the only real African associated with Crawford at this point. He was evidently born a Taureg and taken to the States at an early age, three or four, by a missionary. At any rate, he was educated at the University of Minnesota where he studied political science. We have no record of where he stands politically, but Comrade Baker rated him as an outstanding intuitive soldier. A veritable genius in combat. He would seem to have had military experience somewhere, but we have no record of it. Our Bey-ag-Akhamouk seems somewhat of a mystery man."

The Russian sorted out another sheet. "Kenneth Ballalou, born in Louisiana, educated in Chicago. Another young man but evidently as capable as the others. He seems to be quite a linguist. So far as we know, he holds no political stand whatsoever."

Menzhinsky pursed his lips before saying, "The Isobel Cunningham I mentioned worked with the Africa for Africans Association with two colleagues, a Jacob Armstrong and Clifford Jackson. It is possible that these two, as well as Isobel Cunningham, have joined El Hassan. If so, we will have to check further upon them, although I understand Armstrong is rather elderly and hardly effective under the circumstances."

The man called Anton said evenly, "And this former comrade, Isobel Cunningham, has evidently joined with Crawford even though he . . . was the cause of Abe Baker's death?"

"Evidently."

The Negro's eyes narrowed.

The other said, "And evidently she is a most intelligent and attractive young lady. We had rather high hopes for her formerly."

The Negro party member came to his feet and gathered up the sheaf of papers from the desk. "All right," he said. "Is there anything else?"

The espionage chief shook his head. "You do not need a step by step blueprint, Anton, that is why you have been chosen for this assignment. You are strongly based in Party doctrine. You know what is needed, we can trust you to carry on the Party's aims." After a pause, the Russian added, "Without being diverted by personal feelings."

Anton looked him in the face. "Of course," he said.

Fredric Ostrander was on the carpet.

His chief said, "You seem to have conducted yourself rather precipitately, Fred."

Ostrander shrugged in irritation. "I didn't have time to consult anyone. By pure luck, I spotted the Cunningham girl and since I knew she had affiliated herself with Crawford, I followed her."

The chief said dryly, "And tried to arrest the seven of them, all by yourself."

"I couldn't see anything else to do."

The C.I.A. official said, "In the first place, we have no legal jurisdiction here and you could have caused an international stink. The Russkies would just love to bring something like this onto the Reunited Nations floor. In the second place, you failed. How in the world did you expect to take on that number of men, especially Crawford and his team?"

Ostrander flushed his irritation. "Next time . . ." he began.

His chief waved a hand negatively. "Let's hope there isn't going to be next time, of this type." He took up a paper from his desk. "Here's your new job, Fred. You're to locate this El Hassan and keep in continual contact with him. If he meets with any sort of success at all, and frankly our agency doubts that he will, you will attempt to bring home to Crawford and his followers the fact that they are Americans, and orientate them in the direction of the West. Above all, you are to keep in touch with us and keep us informed on all developments. Especially notify us if there is any sign that our El Hassan is in communication with the Russkies or any other foreign element."

"Right," Ostrander said.

His chief looked at him. "We're giving you this job, Fred, because you're more up on it than anyone else. You're in at the beginning, so to speak. Now, do you want me to assign you a couple of assistants?"

"White men?" Ostrander said.

His higher-up scowled. "You know you're the only Negro in our agency, Fred."

Fredric Ostrander, his voice still even, said, "That's too bad, because anyone you assigned me who wasn't a Negro would be a hindrance rather than an assistant."

The other drummed his fingers on the table in irritation. He said suddenly, "Fred, do you think I ought to do a report to Greater Washington suggesting they take more Negro operatives into the agency?"

Ostrander said dryly, "You'd better if this department is going to get much work done in Africa." He stood up. "I suppose that the sooner I get onto the job, the better. Do you have any idea at all where Crawford and his gang headed after they left me unconscious in that filthy hut?"

"No, we haven't the slightest idea of where they might be, other than that they left your car abandoned at the Yoff airport."

"Oh, great," Fredric Ostrander complained. "They've gone into hiding in an area somewhat twice the size of the original fifty United States."

"Good luck," his chief said.

Rex Donaldson, formerly of Nassau in the British Bahamas, formerly of the College of Anthropology, Oxford, now field man for the African Department of the British Commonwealth working at expediting native development, was taking time out for needed and unwonted relaxation. In fact, he stretched out on his back in the most comfortable bed, in the most comfortable hotel, in the Niger town of Mopti. His hands were behind his head, and his scowling eyes were on the ceiling.

He was a small, bent man, inordinately black even for the Sudan and the loincloth costume he wore was ludicrous in the Westernized comfort of the hotel room. He was attired for the bush and knew that it was sheer laziness now that kept him from taking off for the Dogon country of the Canton de Sangha where he was currently working to bring down tribal prejudices against the coming of the schools. He had his work cut out for him in the Dogon, the old men, the tribal elders they called Hogons, instinctively knew that the coming of education meant subversion of their institutions and the eventual loss of Hogon power.

His portable communicator, sitting on the bedside table, buzzed and the little man grumbled a profanity and swung his crooked legs around to the floor. His eyebrows went up when he realized it was a priority call which probably meant from London.

He flicked the reception switch and a girl's face faded onto the screen. She said, "A moment, Mr. Donaldson, Sir Winton wants you."

"Right," Rex Donaldson said. Sir Winton, yet. Head of the African Department. Other than photographs, Donaldson had never seen his ultimate superior, not to mention speaking to him personally.

The girl's face faded out and that of Sir Winton Brett-Homes faded in. The heavy-set, heavy-faced Englishman looked down, obviously checking something on his desk. He looked up again, said, "Rex Donaldson?"

"Yes, sir."

"I won't waste time on preliminaries, Donaldson. We've been discussing, here, some of the disconcerting rumors coming out of your section. Are you acquainted with this figure, El Hassan?"

The black man's eyes widened. He said, cautiously, "I have heard a good many stories and rumors."

"Yes, of course. They have been filtering into this office for more than a year. But thus far little that could be considered concrete has developed."

Rex Donaldson held his peace, waited for the other to go on.

Sir Winton said impatiently, "Actually, we are still dealing with rumors, but they are beginning to shape up. Evidently, this El Hassan has finally begun to move."

"Ahhh," the wiry little field man breathed.

The florid faced Englishman said, "As we understand it, he wishes to cut across tribal, national and geographic divisions in all North Africa, wishes to unite the whole area from Sudan to the Mediterranean."

"Yes," Donaldson nodded. "That seems to be his program."

Sir Winton said, "It has been decided that the interests of Her Majesty's government and that of the Commonwealth hardly coincide with such an attempt at this time. It would lead to chaos."

"Ahhh," Donaldson said.

Sir Winton wound it up, all but beaming. "Your instructions, then, are to seek out this El Hassan and combat his efforts with whatever means you find necessary. We consider you one of our most competent operatives, Donaldson."

Rex Donaldson said slowly, "You mean that he is to be stopped at all cost?"

The other cleared his throat. "You are given carte blanche, Donaldson. You and our other operatives in the Sahara and Sudan. Stop Al Hassan."

Rex Donaldson said flatly, "You have just received my resignation, Sir Winton."

"What . . . what!"

"You heard me," Donaldson said.

"But . . . but what are you going to do?" The heavy face of the African Department head was going a reddish-purple, which rather fascinated Donaldson but he had no time to further contemplate the phenomenon.

"I'm going to round up a few of my colleagues, of similar mind to my own, and then I'm going to join El Hassan," the little man snapped. "Good-bye, Sir Winton."

He clicked the set off and then looked down at it. His dour face broke into a rare grin. "Now there's an ambition I've had for donkey's years," he said aloud. "To hang up on a really big mucky-muck."

IV

Following the attack of the unidentified rocketcraft, El Hassan's party was twice again nearly flushed by reconnoitering planes of unknown origin. They weren't making the time they wanted.

Beneath a projecting rock face over a gravel bottomed wadi, the two hover-lorries were hidden, whilst a slow-moving helio-jet made sweeping, high-altitude circlings above them.

The six stared glumly upward.

Cliff Jackson who was on the radio called out, "I just picked him up. He's called in to Fort Lamy reporting no luck. His fuel's running short and he'll be knocking off soon."

Homer Crawford rapped, "What language?"

"French," Cliff said, "but it's not his. I mean he's not French, just using the language."

Bey's face was as glum as any and there was a tic at the side of his mouth. He said now, "We've got to come up with something. Sooner or later one of them will spot us and this next time we won't have any fantastic breaks like Homer being able to knock him off with a Tommy-Noiseless. He'll drop a couple of neopalms and burn up a square mile of desert including El Hassan and his whole crew."

Homer looked at him. "Any ideas, Bey?"

"No," the other growled.

Homer Crawford said, "Any of the rest of you?"

Isobel was frowning, bringing something back. "Why don't we travel at night?"

"And rest during the day?" Homer said.

Kenny said, "Parking where? We just made it to this wadi. If we're caught out in the dunes somewhere when one of those planes shows up, we've had it. You couldn't hide a jackrabbit out there."

But Bey and Homer Crawford were still looking at Isobel.

She said, "I remember a story the Tuaregs used to tell about a raid some of them made back during the French occupation. They stole four hundred camels near Timbuktu one night and headed north. The French weren't worried. The next morning, they simply sent out a couple of aircraft to spot the Tuareg raiders and the camels. Like Kenny said, you couldn't hide a jackrabbit in dune country. But there was nothing to be seen. The French couldn't believe it, but they still weren't really worried. After all a camel herd can travel only thirty or so miles a day. So the next day the planes went out again, circling, circling, but they still didn't spot the thieves and their loot, nor the next day. Well, to shorten it, the Tuareg got their four hundred camels all the way up to Spanish Rio de Oro where they sold them."

She had their staring attention. "How?" Elmer blurted.

"It was simple. They traveled all night and then, at dawn, buried the camels and themselves in the sand and stayed there all day."

Homer said, "I'm sold. Boys, I hope you're in physical trim because there's going to be quite a bit of digging for the next few days."

Cliff groaned. "Some Minister of the Treasury," he complained. "They give him a shovel instead of a bankbook."

Everyone laughed.

Bey said, "Well, I suppose we stay here until nightfall."

"Right," Homer said. "Whose turn is it to pull cook duty?"

Isobel said menacingly, "I don't know whose turn it is, but I know I'm going to do the cooking. After that slumgullion Kenny whipped up yesterday, I'm a perpetual volunteer for the job of chef—strictly in self-defense."

"That was a cruel cut," Kenny protested, "however, I hereby relinquish all my rights to cooking for this expedition."

"And me!"

"And me!"

"O.K.," Homer said, "so Isobel is Minister of the Royal Kitchen." He looked at Elmer Allen. "Which reminds me. You're our junior theoretician. Are we a monarchy?"

Elmer Allen scowled sourly and sat down, his back to the wadi wall. "I wouldn't think so."

Isobel went off to make coffee in the portable galley in the rear of the second hovercraft. The others brought forth tobacco and squatted or sat near the dour Jamaican. Years in the desert had taught them the nomad's ability to relax completely given opportunity.

"So if it's not a monarchy, what'll we call El Hassan?" Kenny demanded.

Elmer said slowly, thoughtfully, "We'll call him simply El Hassan. Monarchies are of the past, and El Hassan is the voice of the future, something new. We won't admit he's just a latter-day tyrant, an opportunist seizing power because it's there crying to be seized. Actually, El Hassan is in the tradition of Genghis Khan, Tamerlane, or, more recently, Napoleon. But he's a modern version, and we're not going to hang the old labels on him."

Isobel had brought the coffee. "I think you're right," she said.

"Sold," Homer agreed. "So we aren't a monarchy. We're a tyranny." His face had begun by expressing amusement, but that fell off. He added, "As a young sociologist, I never expected to wind up a literal tyrant." Elmer Allen said, "Wait a minute. See if I can remember this. Comes from Byron." He closed his eyes and recited:

"The tyrant of the Chersonese Was freedom's best and bravest friend. That tyrant was Miltiades, Oh that the present hour would lend Another despot of the kind. Such bonds as his were sure to bind."

Isobel, pouring coffee, laughed and said, "Why Elmer, who'd ever dream you read verse, not to speak of memorizing it, you old sourpuss."

Elmer Allen's complexion was too dark to register a flush.

Homer Crawford said, "Yeah, Miltiades. Seized power, whipped the Athenians into shape to the point where they were able to take the Persians at Marathon, which should have been impossible." He looked around at the others, winding up with Elmer. "What happened to Miltiades after Marathon and after the emergency was over?"

Elmer looked down into his coffee. "I don't remember," he lied.

There was a clicking from the first hover-lorry, and Cliff Jackson put down his coffee, groaned his resentment at fate, and made his way to the vehicle and the radio there.

Bey motioned with his head. "That's handy, our still being able to tune in on the broadcasts the African Development Project makes to its teams."

Kenny said, "Not that what they've been saying is much in the way of flattery."

Bey said, "They seem to think we're somewhere in the vicinity of Bidon Cinq."

"That's what worries me," Homer growled. He raked his right hand back through his short hair. "If they think we're in Southern

Algeria, what are these planes doing around here? We're hundreds of miles from Bidon Cinq."

Bey shot him an oblique glance. "That's easy. That plane that tried to clobber us, and these others that have been trying to search us out, aren't really Reunited Nations craft. They're someone else."

They all looked at him. "Who?" Isobel said.

"How should I know? It could be almost anybody with an iron in the North African fire. The Soviet Complex? Very likely. The British Commonwealth or the French Community? Why not? There're elements in both that haven't really accepted giving up the old colonies and would like to regain them in one way or the other. The Arab Union? Why comment? Common Europe? Oh, Common Europe would love to have a free hand exploiting North Africa."

"You haven't mentioned the United States of the Americas," Elmer said dryly. "I hope you haven't any prejudices in favor of the land of your adoption, Mr. Minister of War."

Bey shrugged. "I just hadn't got around to her. Admittedly with the continued growth of the Soviet Complex and Common Europe, the States have slipped from the supreme position they occupied immediately following the Second War. The more power-happy elements are conscious of the ultimate value of control of Africa and doubly conscious of the danger of it falling into the hands of someone else. Oh, never fear, those planes that have been pestering us might belong to anybody at all."

Cliff Jackson hurried back from his radio, his face anxious. "Listen," he said. "That was a high priority flash, to all Reunited Nations teams. The Arab Union has just taken Tamanrasset. They pushed two columns out of Libya, evidently one from Ghat and one from further north near Ghadamès."

Homer Crawford was on his feet, alert. "Well . . . why?"

Cliff had what amounted to accusation on his face. "Evidently, the El Hassan rumors are spreading like wildfire. There've been more riots in Mopti, and the Reunited Nations buildings in Adrar have been stormed by mobs demonstrating for him. The Arab Union is moving in on the excuse of protecting the country against El Hassan."

Kenny Ballalou groaned, "They'll have half their Arab Legion in here before the week's out."

Cliff finished with, "The Reunited Nations is throwing a wingding. Everybody running around accusing and threatening, and, as per usual, getting nowhere."

Homer Crawford's face was working in thought. He shook his head at Kenny. "I think you're wrong. They won't send the whole Arab Legion in. They'll be afraid to. They'll want to see first what everybody else does. They know they can't stand up to a slugging match with any of the really big powers. They'll stick it out for a while and watch developments. We have, perhaps, two weeks in which to operate."

"Operate?" Cliff demanded. "What do you mean, operate?"

Homer's eyes snapped to him. "I mean to recapture Taman-rasset from the Arab Union, seize the radio and television station there, and proclaim El Hassan's regime."

The big Californian's eyes bugged at him. "You mean the six of us? There'll be ten thousand of them."

"No," Homer said decisively. "Nothing like that number. Possibly a thousand, if that many. Logistics simply doesn't allow a greater number, not on such short notice. They've put a thousand or so of their crack troops into the town. No more."

Cliff wailed, "What's the difference between a thousand and twenty thousand, so far as five men and a girl are concerned?"

The rest were saying nothing, but following the debate.

Crawford explained, not to just Cliff but to all of them. "Actually, the Arab Union is doing part of our job for us. They've openly declared that El Hassan is attempting to take over North Africa, that he's raising the tribes. Well, good. We didn't have the facilities to make the announcement ourselves. But now the whole world knows it."

"That's right," Elmer said, his face characteristically sullen. "Every news agency in the world is playing up the El Hassan story. In a matter of days, the most remote nomad encampment in the Sahara will know of it, one way or the other."

Homer Crawford was pacing, socking his right fist into the palm of the left. "They've given us a rallying raison d'etre. These people might be largely Moslem, especially in the north, but they have no love for the Arab Union. For too long the slave raiders came down from the northeast. Given time, Islam might have moved in on the whole of North Africa. But not this way, not in military columns."

He swung to Bey. "You worked over in the Teda country, before joining my team, and speak the Sudanic dialects. Head for there, Bey. Proclaim El Hassan. Organize a column. We'll rendez-vous at Tamanrasset in exactly two weeks."

Bey growled, "How am I supposed to get to Faya?"

"You'll have to work that out yourself. Tonight we'll drop you near In Guezzam, they have one of the big solar pump, afforesta-tion developments there. You should be able to, ah, requisition a truck, or possibly even a 'copter or aircraft. You're on your own, Bey."

"Right."

Homer spun to Kenny Ballalou. "You're the only one of us who gets along in the dialect of Hassania. Get over to Nemadi country and raise a column. There are no better scouts in the world. Two weeks from today at Tamanrasset."

"Got it. Drop me off tonight with Bey, we'll work together until we liberate some transport."

Bey said, "It might be worth while scouting in In Guezzam for a day or two. We might pick up a couple of El Hassan followers to help us along the way."

"Use your judgment. Elmer!"

Elmer groaned sourly, "I knew my time'd come."

"Up into Chaambra country for you. Take the second lorry. You've got a distance to go. Try to recruit former members of the French Camel Corps. Promise just about anything, but only re-member that one day we'll have to keep the promises. El Hassan can't get the label of phony hung on him."

"Chaambra country," Elmer said. "Oh great. Arabs. I can just see what luck I'm going to have rousing up Arabs to fight other Arabs, and me with a complexion black as . . ."

Homer snapped at him, "They won't be following you, they'll be following El Hassan . . . or at least the El Hassan dream. Play up the fact that the Arab Union is largely not of Africa but of the Middle East. That they're invading the country to swipe the goats and violate the women. Dig up all the old North African preju-dices against the Syrians and Egyptians, and the Saudi-Arabian slave traders. You'll make out."

Cliff said, nervously, "How about me, Homer?"

Homer looked at him. Cliff Jackson, in spite of his fabulous build, hadn't a fighting man's background.

Homer grinned and said, "You'll work with me. We're going into Tuareg country. Whenever occasion calls for it, whip off that shirt and go strolling around with that overgrown chest of yours stuck out. The Tuareg consider themselves the best physical specimens in the Sahara, which they are. They admire masculine physique. You'll wow them."

Cliff grumbled, "Sounds like vaudeville."

Isobel said softly, "And me, El Hassan? What do I do?"

Homer turned to her. "You're also part of headquarters staff. The Tuareg women aren't dominated by their men. They still have a strong element of descent in the matrilinear line and women aren't second-class citizens. You'll work on pressuring them. Do you speak Tamaheq?"

"Of course."

Homer Crawford looked up into the sky, swept it. The day was rapidly coming to an end and nowhere does day become night so quickly as in the ergs of the Sahara.

"Let's get underway," Crawford said. "Time's a wastin'."

The range of the Ahaggar Tuareg was once known, under French administration, as the Annexe du Hoggar, and was the most difficult area ever subdued by French arms—if it was ever subdued. At the battle of Tit on May 7, 1902 the Camel Corps, under Cottenest, broke the combined military power of the Tuareg confederations, but this meant no more than that the tribes and clans carried on nomadic warfare in smaller units.

The Ahaggar covers roughly an area the size of Pennsylvania, New York, Virginia and Maryland combined, and supports a population of possibly twelve thousand, which includes about forty-five hundred Tuareg, four thousand Negro serf-slaves, and some thirty-five hundred scorned sedentary Haratin workers. The balance of the population consists of a handful of Enaden smiths and a small number of Arab shopkeepers in the largest of the sedentary centers. Europeans and other whites are all but unknown.

It is the end of the world.

Contrary to Hollywood inspired belief, the Sahara does not consist principally of sand dunes, although these, too, are present, and all but impassable even to camels. Traffic, through the millennia, has held to the endless stretches of gravelly plains and the rock ribbed plateaus which cover most of the desert. The great sandy wastes or ergs cover roughly a fifth of the entire Sahara, and possibly two thirds of this area consists of the rolling sandy plains dotted occasionally with dunes. The remaining third, or about one fifteenth of the total Sahara, is characterized by the dune formations of popular imagination.

It was through this latter area that Homer Crawford, now with but one hover-lorry, and accompanied by Isobel Cunningham and Clifford Jackson, was heading.

For although the spectacular major dune formations of the Great Erg have defied wheeled vehicles since the era of the Carthaginian chariots, and even the desert born camel limits his daily travel in them to but a few miles, the modern hovercraft, atop its air cushion jets, finds them of only passing difficulty to traverse. And the hovercraft leaves no trail.

Cliff Jackson scowled out at the identical scenery. Identical for more than two hundred miles. For twice that distance, they had seen no other life. No animal, no bird, not a sprig of cactus. This was the Great Erg.

He muttered, "This country is so dry even the morning dew is dehydrated."

Isobel laughed—she, too, had never experienced this country before. "Why, Cliff, you made a funny!"

They were sitting three across in the front seat, with Homer Crawford at the wheel, and now all three were dressed in the costume of the Kel Rela tribe of the Ahaggar Tuareg confederation. In the back of the lorry were the jerrycans of water and the supplies that meant the difference between life and mumification from sun and heat.

Cliff turned suddenly to the driver. "Why here?" he said bitterly. "Why pick this for a base of operations? Why not Mopti? Ten thousand Sudanese demonstrated for El Hassan there less than two weeks ago. You'd have them in the palm of your hand."

Homer didn't look up from his work at wheel, lift and acceleration levers. To achieve maximum speed over the dunes, you worked constantly at directing motion not only horizontally but vertically.

He said, "And the twenty and one enemies of the El Hassan movement would have had us in their palms. Our followers in Mopti can take care of themselves. If this movement is ever going to be worth anything, the local characters are going to have to get into the act. The current big thing is not to allow El Hassan and his immediate troupe to be eliminated before full activities can get under way. For the present, we're hiding out until we can gather forces enough to free Tamanrasset."

"Hiding out is right," Cliff snorted. "I have a sneaking suspicion that not only will they never find us, but we'll never find them again."

Homer laughed. "As a matter of fact, we're not so far right now from Silet where there's a certain amount of water—if you dig for it—and a certain amount of the yellowish grass and woody shrubs that the bedouin depend on. With luck, we'll find the Amenokal of the Tuareg there."

"Amenokal?"

"Paramount chief of the Ahaggar Tuaregs."

The dunes began to fall away and with the butt of his left hand Crawford struck the acceleration lever. He could make more time now when less of his attention was drawn to the ups and downs of erg travel.

Patches of thorny bush began to appear, and after a time a small herd of gazelle were flushed and high tailed their way over the horizon.

Isobel said, "Who is this Amenokal you mentioned?"

"These are the real Tuareg, the comparatively untouched. They've got three tribes, the Kel Rela, the Tégéhé Mellet and the Taitoq, each headed by a warrior clan which gives its name to the tribe as a whole. The chief of the Kel Rela clan is also chief of the Kel Rela tribe and automatically paramount chief, or Amenokal, of the whole confederation. His name is Melchizedek."

"Do you think you can win him over?" Isobel said.

"He's a smart old boy. I had some dealings with him over a year ago. Gave him a TV set in the way of a present, hoping he'd tune in on some of our Reunited Nations propaganda. He's probably the most conservative of the Tuareg leaders."

Her eyebrows went up. "And you expect to bring him around to the most liberal scheme to hit North Africa since Hannibal?"

He looked at her from the side of his eyes and grinned. "Remember Roosevelt, the American president?"

"Hardly."

"Well, you've read about him. He came into office at a time when the country was going to economic pot by the minute. Some of the measures he and his so-called brain trust took were immediately hailed by his enemies as socialistic. In answer, Roosevelt told them that in times of social stress the true conservative is a liberal, since to preserve, you have to reform. If Roosevelt hadn't done the things he did, back in the 1930s, you probably would have seen some real changes in the American socio-economic system. Roosevelt didn't undermine the social system of the time, he preserved it."

"Then, according to you, Roosevelt was a conservative," she said mockingly.

Crawford laughed. "I'll go even further," he said. "When social changes are pending and for whatever reason are not brought about, then reaction is the inevitable alternative. At such a time then—when sweeping socio-economic change is called for—any reform measures proposed are concealed measures of reaction, since they tend to maintain the status quo."

"Holy Mackerel," Cliff protested. "Accept that and Roosevelt was not only not a liberal, but a reactionary. Stop tearing down my childhood heroes."

Isobel said, "Let's get back to this Amenokal guy. You think he's smart enough to see his only chance is in going along with . . ."

Homer Crawford pointed ahead and a little to the right. "We'll soon find out. This is a favorite encampment of his. With luck, he'll be there. If we can win him over, we've come a long way."

"And if we can't?" Isobel said, her eyebrows raised again.

"Then it's unfortunate that there are only three of us," Homer said simply, without looking at her.

There were possibly no more than a hundred Tuareg in all in the nomad encampment of goat leather tents when the solar powered hovercraft drew up.

When the air cushion vehicle stopped before the largest tent, Crawford said beneath his breath, "The Amenokal is here, all right. Cliff, watch your teguelmoust. If any of these people see more than your eyes, your standing has dropped to a contemptible zero."

The husky Californian secured the lightweight cotton, combination veil and turban well up over his face. Earlier, Crawford had shown him how to wind the ten-foot long, indigo-blue cloth around the head and features.

Isobel, of course, was unveiled, Tuareg fashion, and wore baggy trousers of black cotton held in place with a braided leather cord by way of drawstring and a gandoura upper-garment consisting of a huge rectangle of cloth some seven to eight feet square and folded over on itself with the free corners sewed together so as to leave bottom and most of both sides open. A V-shaped opening for her head and neck was cut out of a fold at the top, and a large patch had been sewed inside to make a pocket beneath her left breast. She wasn't exactly a Parisian fashion plate.

Even as they stepped down from the hovercraft, immediately after it had drifted to rest on the ground, an elderly man came from the tent entrance.

He looked at them for a moment, then rested his eyes exclusively on Homer Crawford.

"La Bas, El Hassan," he said through the cloth that covered his mouth.

Homer Crawford was taken aback, but covered the fact. "There is no evil," he repeated the traditional greeting. "But why do you name me El Hassan?"

A dozen veiled desert men, all with the Tuareg sword, several with modern rifles, had formed behind the Tuareg chief.

Melchizedek made a movement of hand to mouth, in a universal gesture of amusement. "Ah, El Hassan," he said, "you forget you left me the magical instrument of the Roumi."

Crawford was mystified, but he stood in silence. What the Tuareg paramount chief said now made considerable difference. As he recalled his former encounter with the Ahaggar leader, the other had been neither friendly nor antagonistic to the Reunited Nations team Crawford had headed in their role as itinerant desert smiths.

The Amenokal said, "Enter then my tent, El Hassan, and meet my chieftains. We would confer with you."

The first obstacle was cleared. Subduing a sigh of relief, Homer Crawford turned to Cliff. "This, O Amenokal of all the Ahaggar, is Clif ben Jackson, my Vizier of Finance."

The Amenokal bowed his head slightly, said, "La Bas."

Cliff could go that far in the Tuareg tongue. He said, "La Bas."

The Amenokal said, looking at Isobel, "I hear that in the lands of the Roumi women are permitted in the higher councils."

Homer said steadily, "This I have also been amazed to hear.

However, it is fitting that my followers remain here while El Hassan discusses matters of the highest importance with the Amenokal and his chieftains. This is the Sitt Izubahil, high in the councils of her people due to the great knowledge she has gained by attending the new schools which dispense rare wisdom, as all men know."

The Amenokal courteously said, "La Bas," but Isobel held her peace in decency amongst men of chieftain rank.

When Homer and the Tuaregs had disappeared into the tent, she said to Cliff, "Stick by the car, I'm going to circulate among the women. Women are women everywhere. I'll pick up the gossip, possibly get something Homer will miss in there."

A group of Tuareg women and children, the latter stark naked, had gathered to gape at the strangers. Isobel moved toward them, began immediately breaking the ice.

Under his breath, Cliff muttered, "What a gal. Give her a few hours and she'll form a Lady's Aid branch, or a bridge club, and where else is El Hassan going to pick up so much inside information?"

The tent, which was of the highly considered mouflon skins, was mounted on a wooden frame which consisted of two uprights with a horizontal member laid across their tops. The tent covering was stretched over this framework with its back and sides pegged down and the front, which faced south, was left open. It was ten feet deep, fifteen feet wide and five feet high in the middle.

The men entered and filed to the right of the structure where sheepskins and rugs provided seating. The women and children, who abided ordinarily to the left side, had vanished for this gathering of the great.

They sat for a time and sipped at green tea, syrup sweet with mint and sugar, the tiny cups held under the teguelmoust so as not to obscenely reveal the mouth of the drinker.

Finally, Homer Crawford said, "You spoke of the magical instrument of the Roumi which I gave you as gift, O Amenokal, and named me El Hassan."

Several of the Tuareg chuckled beneath their veils but Crawford could read neither warmth nor antagonism in their amusement.

The elderly Melchizedek nodded. "At first we were bewildered, O El Hassan, but then my sister's son, Guémama, fated perhaps one day to become chief of the Kel Rela and Amenokal of all the Ahaggar, recalled the tales told by the storytellers at the fire in the long evenings."

Crawford looked at him politely.

Melchizedek's laugh was gentle. "But each man has heard, in his time, O El Hassan, of the ancient Calif Haroun El Raschid of Baghdad."

Crawford's mind went into high gear, as the story began to come back to him. From second into high gear, and he could have blessed these bedouin for handing him a piece of publicity gobbledygook worthy of Fifth Avenue's top agency.

He held up a hand as though in amusement at being discovered. "Wallahi, O Amenokal, you have discovered my secret. For many months I have crossed the deserts disguised as a common Enaden smith to seek out all the people and to learn their wishes and their needs."

"Even as Haroun el Raschid in the far past," one of the subchiefs muttered in satisfaction, "used to disguise himself as a lowborn dragoman and wander the streets of Baghdad."

"But how did you recognize me?" Homer said.

The Amenokal said in reproof, "But verily, your name is on all lips. The Roumi have branded you common criminal. You are to be seized on sight and great reward will be given he who delivers you to the authorities." He spoke without inflection, and Crawford could read neither support nor animosity—nor greed for the reward offered by El Hassan's enemies. He gathered the impression that the Tuareg chief was playing his cards close to his chest.

"And what else do they say?"

The elderly Melchizedek went on slowly, "They say that El Hassan is in truth a renegade citizen of a far away Roumi land and that he attempts to build a great confederation in North Africa for his own gain."

One of the others chuckled and said, "The Roumi on the magical instrument are indeed great liars as all can see."

Homer looked at him questioningly.

The other said, laughing, "Who has ever heard of a black Roumi? And you, O El Hassan, are as black as a Bela."

The Amenokal finished off the mystery of Crawford's recognition. "Know, El Hassan, that whilst you were here before, one of the slaves that served you for pay shamelessly looked upon your face in the privacy of your tent. It was this slave who recognized your face when the Roumi presented it on the magic instrument, calling upon all men to see you and to brand you enemy."

So that was it. The Reunited Nations, and probably all the rest, had used their radio and TV stations to broadcast a warning and offer a reward for Homer and his followers. Old Sven was losing no time. This wasn't so good. A Tuareg owes allegiance to no one beyond clan, tribe and confederation. All others are outside the pale and any advantage, monetary or otherwise, to be gained by exploiting a stranger is well within desert mores.

He might as well bring it to the point. Crawford said evenly, "And I have entered your camp alone except for two followers. Your people are many. So why, O Amenokal, have you not seized me for the reward the Roumi offer?"

There was a moment of silence and Homer Crawford sensed that the subchieftains had leaned forward in anticipation, waiting for their leader's words. Possibly they, too, could not understand.

The Tuareg leader finished his tea.

"Because, El Hassan, we yet have not heard the message which the Roumi are so anxious that you not be allowed to bring the men of the desert. The Roumi are great liars, and great thieves, as each man knows. In the memory of those still living, they have stolen of the bedouin and robbed him of land and wealth. So now we would hear of what you say, before we decide."

"Spoken like a true Amenokal, a veritable Suliman ben Davud," Homer said with a heartiness he could only partly feel. At least they were open to persuasion.

For a long moment he stared down at the rug upon which they sat, as though deep in contemplation.

"These words I speak will be truly difficult to hear and accept, O men of the veil," he said at last. "For I speak of great change, and no man loves change in the way of his life."

"Speak, El Hassan," Melchizedek said flatly. "Great change is everywhere upon us, as each man knows, and none can tell how to maintain the ways of our fathers."

"We can fight," one of the younger men growled.

The Amenokal turned to him and grunted scorn. "And would you fight against the weapons of the djinn and afrit, O Guémama? Know that in my youth I was distant witness to the explosion of a great weapon which the accursed Franzawi discharged south of

Reggan. Know, that this single explosion, my sister's son, could with ease have destroyed the total of all the tribesmen of the Ahaggar, had they been gathered."

"And the Roumi have many such weapons," Crawford added gently.

The eyes of the tribal headmen came back to him.

"As each man knows," Crawford continued, "change is upon the world. No matter how strongly one wills to continue the traditions of his fathers, change is upon us all. And he who would press against the sand storm, rather than drifting with it, lasts not long."

One of the subchiefs growled, "We Tuareg love not change, El Hassan."

Crawford turned to him. "That is why I and my viziers have spent long hours in ekhwan, in great council, devoted to the problems of the Tuareg and how they can best fit into the new Africa that everywhere awakes."

They stirred in interest now. The Tuareg, once the Scourge of the Sahara, the Sons of Shaitan and the Forgotten of Allah, to the Arab, Teda, Moroccan and other fellow inhabitants of North Africa, were of recent decades developing a tribal complex. Robbed of their nomadic-bandit way of life by first the French Camel Corps and later by the efforts of the Reunited Nations, they were rapidly descending into a condition of poverty and defensive bewilderment. Not only were large numbers of former bedouin drifting to the area's sedentary centers, an act beyond contempt within the memory of the elders, but the best elements of the clans were often deserting Tuareg country completely and defecting to the new industrial centers, the dam projects, the afforestation projects, the new oases irrigated with the solar-powered pumps.

"Speak, El Hassan," the Amenokal ordered. And unconsciously, he, too, leaned forward, as did his subchiefs. The Ahaggar Tuareg were reaching for straws, unconsciously seeking shoulders upon which to lay their unsolvable problems.

"Let me, O chiefs of the Tuareg, tell of a once strong tribe of warriors and nomads who lived in the far country in which I was born," Crawford said. The desert man loves a story, a parable, a tale of the strong men of yesteryear.

Melchizedek clapped his hands in summons and when a slave appeared, called for narghileh water pipes. When all had been supplied, they relaxed, bits in mouths and looked again at Homer

Crawford.

"They were called," he intoned, "the Cheyenne. The Northern Cheyenne, for they had a sister tribe to the South. And on all the plains of this great land, a land, verily, as large as all that over which the Tuareg confederations now roam, they were the greatest huntsmen, the greatest warriors. All feared them. They were the lords of all."

"Ai," breathed one of the older men. "As were the Tuareg before the coming of the cursed Franzawi and the other Nazrani."

"But in time," Crawford pursued, "came the new ways to the plains, and these men who lived largely by the chase began to see the lands fenced in for farmers, began to see large cities erected on what were once tribal areas, and to see the iron railroads of the new ways begin to spread out over the whole of the territory which once was roamed only by the Cheyennes and such nomadic tribes."

"Ai," a muffled mouth ejected.

Homer Crawford looked at the younger Targui, Guémama, the Amenokul's nephew. "And so," he said, "they fought."

"Wallahi!" Guémama breathed.

Homer Crawford looked about the circle. "Never has tribe fought as did the Cheyenne. Never has the world seen such warriors, with the exception, of course, of the Ahaggar Tuareg. Never were such raids, never such bravery, never such heroic deeds as were performed by the warriors of the Cheyennes and their women, and their old people and their children. Over and over they defeated the cavalry and the infantry of the newcomers who would change the old ways and bring the new to the lands of the Cheyennes."

The bedouin were staring in fascination, their water pipes forgotten.

"And then . . . ?" the Amenokal demanded.

"The new ways taught the enemy how to make guns, and artillery, and finally Gatling guns, which today we call machine guns. And once a brave warrior might prevail against a common man armed with the weapons of the new ways, and even twice he might. But the numbers of the followers of the new ways are as the sands of the Great Erg and in time bravery means nothing."

"It is even so," someone growled. "They are as the sands of the erg, and they have the weapons of the djinn, as each man knows."

"And what happened in the end, O El Hassan?"

His eyes swept them all. "They perished," Homer said. "Today in all the land where once the Cheyenne pursued the game there is but a handful of the tribe alive. And they have become nothing people, no longer warriors, no longer nomads, and they are scorned by all for they are poor, poor, poor. Poor in mind and spirits, and in property and they have not been able to adjust to the ways of the new world."

Air went out of the lungs of the assembled Tuareg.

The Amenokal looked at him. "This is verily the truth, El Hassan?"

"My head upon it," Crawford said.

"And why do you tell us of these Cheyenne, these great warriors of the plains of the land of your birth? The story fails to bring joy to hearts already heavy with the troubles of the Tuareg."

It was time to play the joker.

Crawford said carefully, "Because there was no need, O Amenokal of all the Ahaggar, for the Cheyenne to disappear before the sandstorm of the future. They could have ridden before it and today occupy a position of honor and affluence in their former land."

They stared at him.

"And give up the old ways?" Guémama demanded. "Become no longer nomads, no longer honorable warriors, but serfs, slaves, working with one's hands upon the land and with the oil-dirty machines of the Roumi?"

The chiefs muttered angrily.

Crawford said hurriedly, "No! Never! In our great conferences, my viziers and I decided that the Tuareg could never so change. The Tuareg must die, as did the Northern Cheyenne before he would become a city dweller, a worker of the land."

"Bismillah!" someone muttered.

"Too often," Crawford explained, "do the bringers of these things of the future, be they Roumi or others, fail to utilize the potential services of the people of the lands they over-sweep."

"I do not understand you, El Hassan," Melchizedek grumbled. "There is no room for the Tuareg in this new world of bringing trees to the desert, of the great trucks which speed across the erg a score of time the pace of a hejin racing camel, of larger and ever larger oases with their great towns, their schools, their new industries. If the Tuareg remains Tuareg, he cannot fit into this new world, it destroys the old traditions, the old way which is the Tuareg way."

Homer Crawford now turned on the pressure. His voice took on overtones of the positive, his personality seemed to reach out and seize them, and even his physical stature seemed to grow.

"Some indeed of the ways of the bedouin must go," he entoned, "but the Tuareg will survive under my leadership. A people who have throve a millennium and more in the great wastes of the Sahara have strong survival characteristics and will blossom, not die, in my new world. Know, O Melchizedek, that it has been decided that the Ahaggar Tuareg will be the heart of my Desert Legion. In times of conflict, armed with the new arms, and riding the new vehicles, they will adapt their old methods of warfare to this new age. In times of peace they will patrol the new forests, watching for fire and other disaster, they will become herdsmen of the new herds and be the police and rescue forces of this wide area. As the Cheyennes of the olden times of the land of my birth could have become herdsmen and forest rangers and have performed similar tasks had they been shown the way."

Homer Crawford let his eyes go from one of them to the next, and his personality continued to dominate them.

The Amenokal ran his thin, aged hand through the length of his white beard beneath his teguelmoust and contemplated this stranger come out of the ergs to lead his people to still greater changes than those they had thus far rebelled against.

Crawford realized that the Targui was divided in opinion and inwardly the American was in a cold sweat. But his voice registered only supreme confidence. "Under my banner, all North Africa will be welded into one. And all the products of the land will be available in profusion to my faithful followers. The finest wheat for cous cous from Algeria and Tunis, the finest dates and fruits from the oases to the north, the manufactured products of the factories of Dakar and Casablanca. For Africa has always been a poor land but will become a rich one with the new machines and techniques that I will bring."

The Amenokal raised a hand to stem the tide of oratory. "And what do you ask of us now, El Hassan?"

Instead of to the older man, Crawford turned his eyes to the face of Guémama, the leader of the young clansmen. "Now my people are gathering to establish the new rule. Teda from the east, Chaambra from the north, Sudanese from the south, Nemadi, Moors and Rifs from the west. We rendezvous in ten days from now at Tamanrasset where the Arab Legion dogs have seized the city as they wish to seize all the lands of the Sahara and Sudan for the corrupt Arab Union politicians."

Crawford came to his feet. His voice took on an edge of command. "You will address your scouts and warriors and each will ride off on the swiftest camels at your command to raise the Tuareg tribes. And the clans of the Kel Rela will unite with the Taitoq and the Tégéhé Mellet in a great harka at this point and we will ride together to sweep the Arab Legion from the lands of El Hassan."

Guémama was on his feet, too. "Bilhana!" he roared. "With joy."

The others were arising in excitement, all but Melchizedek, who still stroked his gray streaked beard beneath his teguelmoust. The Amenokal had seen much of desert war in his day and knew the horror of the new weapons possessed by the crack troops of the Arab Legion.

But his aged shoulders shrugged against the inevitable.

Crawford said, the ring of authority in his voice. "What does the Amenokal of all the Ahaggar say?" He had no intention of antagonizing the Tuareg chief by going over his head and directly to the people.

"Thou art El Hassan," Melchizedek said, his voice low, "and undoubtedly it is fated that the Tuareg follow you, for verily there is no way else to go, as each man knows."

"Wallahi!" Guémama crowed jubilantly.

V

Guémama, nephew of Melchizedek the Amenokal of the Ahaggar Tuareg confederation and fighting chief of the Kel Rela clan of the Kel Rela tribe, brought his Hejin racing camel to an abrupt halt with a smack of his mish'ab camel stick. He barked, "Adar-ya-yan," in command to bring it to its knees, and slid to the ground before his mount had groaned its rocking way to the sand.

The Tarqui was jubilant. His dark eyes sparked above his teguelmoust veil and he presented himself before Homer Crawford with the elan of a Napoleonic cavalryman before his emperor. Were red leather fil fil boots capable of producing a clicking of heels, that sound would have rung.

Crawford said with dignity, "Aselamu, Aleikum, Guémama. Greeting to you."

"Salaam Aleikum," the tribesman got out breathlessly. "Your message spreads, O El Hassan. My men ride to eastward and westward and never a tent from here to Silet, from In Guezzam to Timissao but knows that El Hassan calls. The Taitoq and the Tégéhé Mellet ride!"

Homer Crawford was standing before the hovercraft. The Amenokal's tribesmen had set up two large goat leather tents for his use and the three Americans had largely withdrawn to their shelter. Crawford was aware of the dangers of familiarity.

Cliff Jackson, who as usual had been monitoring the radio, came from the hover-lorry and growled, "What's he saying?"

"The tribesmen are gathering as per instructions," Homer said in English.

Jackson grunted, somewhat self-conscious of the Targui's admiring gaze. The Tuareg is the handsomest physical specimen of North Africa, often going to six foot of wiry manhood, but there was nothing in all the Sahara to rival the build of Homer Crawford, not to speak of the giant Cliff Jackson.

Crawford turned back to the Tuareg chieftain. "You please me well, O Guémama. Know that I have been in conference with my viziers on the Roumi device which enables one to speak great distances and that we have decided that you are to head all the fighting clans of the Ahaggar, and that you will ride at the left hand of El Hassan, as shield on shoulder rides."

The Targui, overwhelmed, made adequate pledges of fidelity,

flowering words of thanks, and then hurried off to inform his fellow tribesmen of his appointment.

Isobel emerged from her tent. She looked at Homer obliquely, the sides of her mouth turning down. "As shield on shoulder rides," she translated from the Tamaheq Berber tongue into English. "Hm-m-m." She cast her eyes upward in memory. "You aren't plagiarizing Kipling, are you?"

Crawford grinned at her. "These people like a well turned phrase."

"And who could turn them better than Rudyard?" she said. Her voice dropped the bantering tone. "What's this bit about making Guémama war-chief of the Tuareg? Isn't he on the young and enthusiastic side?"

Cliff scowled. "You mean that youngster? Why he can't be more than in his early twenties."

Crawford was looking after the young Targui who was disappearing into his uncle's tent on the far side of the rapidly growing encampment.

"You mean the age of Napoleon in the Italian campaign, or Alexander at Issus?" he asked. Isobel began to respond to that, but he shook his head. "He's the Amenokal's nephew, and traditionally would probably get the position anyway. He's the most popular of the young tribesmen, and it's going to be they who do the fighting. Having the appointment come from El Hassan, and at this early point, will just bind him closer. Besides that, he's a natural born warrior. Typical. Enthusiastic, bold, brave and with the military mind."

"What's a military mind?" Cliff said.

"He can take off his shirt without unbuttoning his collar," Homer told him.

"Very funny," Cliff grumbled.

Isobel turned to the big Californian. "What's on the radio, Cliff?"

"Let's go get a cup of coffee," he said. "All hellzapoppin."

They went into the larger of the two Tuareg tents, and Isobel poured water from a girba into the coffee pot which she placed on a heat unit, flicking its switch. She said sarcastically, from the side of her mouth, "A message, O El Hassan, from the Department of Logistics, subdepartment Commissary of Headquarters of the Commander in Chief. Unless you get around to capturing some supplies in the near future, your food is going to be prepared over a camel dung fire. This heat unit is fading out on me."

"Don't bother me with trivialities," Homer told her. "I've got big things on my mind."

She looked at him suspiciously. "Hm-m-m. Such as what?"

"Such as whether to put my face on the postage stamps profile or full."

She said, under her breath, "I shoulda known. Already, delusions of grandeur."

"Holy Mackerel," Cliff protested. "Aren't we ever serious around this place? You two will wind up gagging with the firing squad."

Crawford chuckled softly but let his face go serious. "Sorry, Cliff. What's on your mind?"

Cliff said impatiently, "From the radio reports, the Arab Union is consolidating its position. El Hassan is being discredited by the minute. Your followers were in control for a time in Mopti and Bamako, but they're falling away because of lack of direction. The best way I can put reports together, the Reunited Nations is in complete confusion. Everybody accusing everybody of double-dealing."

Isobel said dryly, "Any other good news?"

Cliff said glumly, "Rumors, rumors, rumors. Half the marabouts in North Africa are proclaiming a jihad in support of the Pan-Islam program of the Arab Union. Listen, Homer, we've got to get the backing of the Moslem leaders."

Homer Crawford grunted. "We need Islam in this part of the world like we need a hole in the head. That's one of the things already wrong with North Africa."

"What's wrong with Islam? It was probably the most dynamic religion ever to sweep the world."

"Was is right," Crawford growled, now on one of his favorite peeve subjects. "The Moslem religion exploded out of Arabia with some new concepts that set the world in ferment from India to Southern France. For all practical purposes Islam invented science. Sure, the Greeks had logic and the Romans had engineering—without applying the Greek-style logic. But the Arabs amalgamated the two concepts to yield experimental science. They were able to take the intellectual products of a dozen cultures and wield them into one. For a hundred years or so it looked as though they had something."

When he hesitated for a moment, Isobel said, questioningly, "And . . ."

"And they couldn't get away from that Q'ran of theirs. They took it seriously. They started off in their big universities, such as those at Fez, being the greatest scientists and scholars the world had ever seen. But the fundamentalists won out, and in a couple of hundred years the only thing being taught at Fez was the Q'ran. To even suggest that all necessary information isn't contained therein, is enough to have you clobbered. Islam became the most reactionary force to suppress progress in the civilized world. In fact, by this period in world history, we don't even think of the Moslem world as particularly civilized."

Cliff said defensively, "The Bible doesn't encourage original thinking either. A fundamentalist . . ."

"Sure," Crawford interrupted. "Those elements who take the Bible the way Islam took the Q'ran wind up in the same rut. But as a whole, Europe was sparked enough by the original Islamic explosion that the Renaissance resulted, with what world results we all know. Be . . ."

There was a roar of confusion outside. A blasting of guns, a shrieking of Ul-Ul-Ul-Allah Akbar!

Crawford came to his feet unhappily. "Another contingent of Tuareg," he said. "I'll have to give them a quick welcoming to the colors speech."

The guns outside continued their booming.

"Confound it," he growled, "I wish I could break them of that habit of blasting away their ammunition. They'll have better targets before the week is out."

He pushed open the tent flap and, followed by Isobel and Cliff, emerged into the stretch of clearing between his tents and the hovercraft, and the growing Tuareg encampment. His diagnosis had been correct. A contingent of possibly two score Tuareg camelmen had come a-galloping up, shaking rifles above their heads in a small scale gymhana, or fantasia as the Moors called them.

"At least it's a larger group than usual," Cliff said from behind. "But at this rate, it'll still take a month for us to equal the Arab Legion in Tamanrasset." He added in disgust, "And look at this bunch of ragamuffins. Half of them are carrying muzzleloaders."

The booming muskets and the cracking rifles suddenly began to fall off in intensity and the camelmen and the hordes of Tuareg women and naked children who had swarmed from the tents to greet them were falling silent. Here and there a hand pointed upward.

Homer, Cliff and Isobel swung their own eyes up to the sky in dreaded anticipation. The hover-lorry was camouflaged to blend in with the sands and rock outcroppings of this area, but it was possible that an aircraft might have determined that this was El Hassan's base, possibly through some act of a traitor, in which case . . .

They found the spot in the sky that the tribesmen were pointing out. It seemed to move slowly for a military craft, but for that matter it might be a heliojet and considerably more dangerous, so far as they being spotted was concerned, than a fast moving fighter.

Guémama, was barking to his men to take cover. Two days before Crawford had checked out several of the more bright-eyed on the flac rifle, and now three of them ran to where it was set up at a high point.

But hardly had the confused milling got under way than it fell off again. Movement stopped, and the Tuareg faced the approaching dot in the sky.

"Djinn . . . !"

"Afrit . . . !"

Cliff had darted back into the tent, now he emerged with binoculars.

"What the devil is it?" Crawford snapped. Desert trained eyes were evidently considerably more effective than his own. He couldn't see what the tribesmen were gaping at.

"It's the smallest heliohopper I've ever seen," Cliff snorted. "It's so small practically all you can see are the rotors and the passenger. He doesn't even look as though he's got a seat."

Guémama came hurrying up, his eyes wide beneath his teguelmoust. "El Hassan! A witchman . . . come out of the sky!"

Homer said evenly, "It is nothing. Only post men ready to obey my commands."

Guémama hesitated as though to waver out another protest, but then spun and hurried off—military-like, glad to have an order to obey to keep his mind from the impossible.

"I'm beginning to have a sneaking suspicion—" Crawford began without finishing. "Come on Isobel, Cliff. We're going to have to make the most of this."

Rex Donaldson, ex-field man for the African Department of the British Commonwealth, dropped the lift lever of his helio-hopper and settled to the ground immediately before Homer Crawford who stood there flanked by Isobel Cunningham and Cliff Jackson. Further back and in the form of a crescent were possibly two or three hundred Tuareg of all ages and both sexes.

Donaldson, in the garb of a Dogan juju man consisting of little more than a wisp of cloth about his loins, played it straight, not knowing the setup. On the face of it, he had just flown out of the sky personally. The size of his equipment so small as to be all but meaningless.

He unstrapped himself from the thin, bicyclelike seat, and, expressionlessly, folded the rotors of his tiny craft back over themselves and the engine, collapsed the whole thing into a manageable packet of some seventy-five pounds, the seat now becoming a handle, and then turned and faced Crawford.

Donaldson screwed his wizened face into an expression of respect and made a motion of obeisance. Then he waited.

Isobel said, "El Hassan bids you speak."

That was the tip-off, then. Crawford had already revealed himself to these people as El Hassan. Very well.

Donaldson spoke in Arabic, not knowing the Tamaheq tongue. "Aselamu, Aleikum, El Hassan. I come to obey your wishes."

A sigh had gone through the Tuareg. "Aiiiii." Wallahi, even the djinn obeyed El Hassan!

With dignity, Homer Crawford said, "Keif halak, all in my house is yours."

Rex Donaldson inclined his small bent body again, in respect.

Crawford said in English, "Let's not carry this too far. Come on into the tent."

Ignoring the Tuareg, who still gaped but held their distance, the four English-speaking Negroes headed for the larger of the two tents that had been set up for El Hassan.

As they passed Guémama who stood slightly aside from the other Tuareg with his uncle Melchizedek, the Amenokal, Crawford nodded and said, speaking to them both. "A messenger from my people to the south. Continue with your newly arrived warriors, O Guémama."

Cliff Jackson had picked up the folded heliohopper and was now carrying it easily.

Guémama looked at the device and blinked.

Crawford refrained from laughing at his commander of irregulars. "It is not a kambu device. My people deal not in magic. It is but one of the many of the things the new ways bring. One day, Guémama," Homer's face remained expressionless, "perhaps you will fly thus."

The teguelmoust hid the other's blanch.

In the tent, Homer turned to the Bahaman, motioned to what seating arrangements were available.

Isobel said, "I'll get some coffee."

Cliff blurted, "Holy Mackerel, if Donaldson, here, can drop in on us out of a clear sky, what keeps anybody else from doing it? Somebody with a couple of neopalm bombs in the way of calling cards."

The dried up little man grimaced in his equivalent of a grin and said, "Hold it, you chaps. I want to notify the others."

"The others? What others?" Crawford said.

Donaldson ignored him for a moment, unslung the small bag he carried over one shoulder and dipped into it for a tiny, two-way radio. He pressed the buzzer button, then held it up to his mouth. "Jack, Jimmy, Dave. Here we are. Took donkey's years, but I found them. You chaps zero-in here." He left the device on and set it to one side, then yawned and settled himself to the rug-covered ground, crosslegged, Dogon style.

Homer Crawford, even as he sat down himself on a footlocker, in lieu of a chair, rapped, "How did you find us? Who did you just radio? Where'd you come from?"

"I say, hold it," Donaldson chuckled sourly. "First of all, I've come to join up. I thought as far back as that time we co-operated in quelling the riots in Mopti that you ought to do this—proclaim yourself El Hassan. When I heard you'd taken the step, I came to join up."

"Oh, great," Cliff said. "What took you so long? We hardly get here, to our ultra-secret hideout, than here you are."

Isobel came with the coffee and handed it around, silently. Then she, too, settled to the rug which covered the sand of the floor.

Rex Donaldson turned to Cliff and there was a wrinkle of amusement in the older man's eyes. "I took so long, because I needed the time to recruit a few other chaps I knew would stand with us."

Crawford rapped, "That's who you just radioed?"

"Of course, old boy. I'd hardly bring the opposition down on us, would I?"

"Where are they?"

"In a couple of hovercraft, similar to your own, possibly twenty kilometers to the southwest."

"You still haven't told us how you found us?"

The little man shrugged. "After tendering my resignation to Sir Winton, I considered the possibilities, which narrowed down very quickly when I heard the Arab Legion had taken Tamanrasset."

"Why?" Isobel said.

Donaldson shot a glance at her. "Because, my dear, unless El Hassan is able to retake Tamanrasset, his movement has come a cropper." He turned his eyes back to Crawford, who was nervously running his hand through his hair. "I knew you had done considerable work in this area, so your whereabouts became obvious seeing that Tamanrasset is in Tuareg country. It was simply a matter of finding what Tuareg encampment was your base, and since your quickest manner of gathering support would be to swing the Amenokal to your banner, I headed for his usual encampment this time of year."

Cliff looked at Homer Crawford. "If Rex found us so easily, so will anybody else."

Isobel put in. "Not necessarily. Mr. Donaldson has information that most of El Hassan's opponents wouldn't."

Homer came to his feet unhappily and began pacing. "No, Isobel. Ostrander, for instance, has all the dope Rex has and is just as capable of working it through to a conclusion. It takes no great insight to realize El Hassan has to either put up or shut up when it comes to Tamanrasset. That's possibly why some of the other elements interested in North Africa have so far refrained from action against the Arab Union. They want to see what El Hassan is going to do—find out just what he has on the ball."

Rex Donaldson looked at him interestedly, "And? What are

your plans?"

Homer Crawford's face worked. "My plans right at present are to stay alive, and you finding me so easily isn't heartening. However, it brings to mind some other problems which need solving, too."

The rest of them fell silent, looking at him. His usual casual humor had dropped away, and his personality gripped them.

He stopped his pacing, and frowned down at them.

"El Hassan is going to have to remain on the move. Always. There can be no capital city, no definite base, and it's going to be a poor idea to sleep twice in the same place." He shook his head emphatically as though to deny rebuttal, which they hadn't actually made. "El Hassan's enemies mustn't know his location within twenty miles."

"Twenty miles!" Cliff blurted.

Crawford stared at him, but unseeingly. "Yes. At least half a dozen of our opponents possess nuclear weapons."

Donaldson demured, sourly. "A nuclear weapon hasn't been exploded for donkey's years and—"

"Of course not," Homer snapped. "Nor would anyone dare, anywhere else except in the wastes of the Sahara. A nuclear explosion in the Ahaggar would not go undetected and a controversy might go up in the Reunited Nations. But who could prove who had done it? And who, actually, would care if in the explosion a common foe of all was eliminated? But let the Arab Union, or possibly the Soviet Complex, or even others, learn definitely where El Hassan is and a bomb could well devastate twenty square miles seeking him out." Crawford shook his head. "No, we've simply got to keep on the move."

Donaldson said, even as he nodded agreement, "And what other problems were you talking about?"

"Oh?" Homer said. "Well, keeping on the move will serve to add mystery to the El Hassan legend. It isn't good for this Tuareg encampment, for instance, to see too much of El Hassan. A leader claiming domination of half a continent looks small potatoes in a desert camp of a few score tents. On the move, showing up here, there, the other place, for only a day or two at a time, is another proposition."

He thought a moment. "Remember DeGaulle?"

"How could we forget?" Rex Donaldson said wryly.

"He had one angle that couldn't be more correct. He said a leader had to keep remote, ever mysterious. He can't afford to have real intimates. Napoleon, Hitler, Stalin. None of them had a real friend to their name. The nearest to friends that Adolph the Aryan ever had, his old comrades of the beerhall days, such as Rhoem, he butchered in the blood purge. And Stalin? He managed to do away with every Old Bolshevik he knew in the days before the Party came to power."

Cliff was staring at him. "Hey," he said. "The one other thing one of these mystical leader types needs is a belief in his own destiny. To the point of clobbering all his intimates if he thinks they stand in his way."

Homer broke into a sudden short laugh. "Any qualms, Cliff?"

Cliff growled, "I don't know. This dream of yours is growing. Where it might end—I don't know."

As they were talking the cries of Ul-Ul-Ul-Allah Akbar! had broken out again.

"Heavens to Betsy," Isobel said. "Another contingent of camelmen?"

But this time the newcomers were three in number and rode in air cushion hover-lorries, the twins of that used by Homer Crawford.

Rex Donaldson brought them up to the tent, saying, "I didn't think you chaps were quite so close."

Homer, Cliff and Isobel faced the new recruits. The three were dressed in khaki bushshirts, shorts and heavy walking shoes—British style. Two were so obviously relatives that they could have been twins except for an age discrepancy of two or three years. They were smaller in stature than the Americans present, almost chunky, but their faces held education and cultivation. The third was slight of build, almost as wiry as Rex Donaldson, and seemed ever at ease.

The small, bent Bahaman made introductions. "Gentlemen, let me present El Hassan—Homer Crawford to you—formerly of the Reunited Nations African Development Project, formerly of the United States of the Americas." His face twisted in his sour grimace of a grin. "Now running for the office of tyrant of North Africa. And these are two of his original and most trusted adherents, Isobel Cunningham and Cliff Jackson." Donaldson turned to the newcomers. "John and James Peters—that's Jack and

Jimmy, of course—recently colleagues of mine with the African Department of the Commonwealth, working largely in the Nigeria area."

Homer shook hands, grinning. "You're a long way from home."

"Farther than that," the one labeled Jack said without a smile changing the seriousness of his face. "We're originally from Trinidad."

Donaldson said, "And this is David Moroka, late of South Africa."

The wiry South African said easily, "Not so very late. In fact, I haven't seen Jo-burg since I was a boy."

He was shaking hands with Isobel now. "Jo-burg?" she said.

"Johannesburg," he translated. "I got out by the skin of my teeth during the troubles in the 1950s."

"You sound like an American," Cliff said when it was his turn to shake.

"Educated in the States," Moroka said. "Best thing that ever happened to me was to be kicked out of the land of my birth."

Homer made a sweeping gesture at the floor and the few articles of furniture the tent contained that could be improvised as chairs. "I'm surprised you're up here instead of in your own neck of the woods," he said to the South African.

Moroka shrugged. "I was considering heading south when I ran into Jimmy and Jack, here. They'd already got the word on the El Hassan movement from Rex. Their arguments made sense to me."

Eyes went to the brothers from Trinidad and Jack Peters took over the position of spokesman. He said, seriously, as though trying to convince the others, "North Africa is the starting point, the beginning. Given El Hassan's success in uniting North Africa, the central areas and later even the south will fall into line. Perhaps one day there will be a union of all Africa."

"Or at least a strong confederation," Jimmy Peters added.

Homer nodded thoughtfully. "Perhaps. But we can't look that far forward now." He looked from one of the newcomers to the other. "I don't know to what extent you fellows understand what the rest of us have set out to accomplish but I suppose if you've been with Rex for the past week, you have a fairly clear idea."

"I believe so," Jack nodded, straight-faced.

Homer Crawford said slowly, "I don't want to give you the wrong idea. If you join up, you'll find it's no parade. Our chances were slim to begin, and we've had some setbacks. As you've probably heard, the Arab Union has stolen a march on us. And from what we can get on the radio, we have thus far to pick up a single adherent among the world powers."

"Powers?" Cliff snorted. "We haven't got a nation the size of Monaco on our side."

Moroka shot a quick glance at the big Californian.

Isobel caught it and laughed. "Cliff's a perpetual sourpuss," she said. "However, he's been in since the first."

The South African looked at her in turn. "We were hardly prepared to find a beautiful American girl in the Great Erg," he said.

Something about his voice caused her to flush. "We've all caught Homer's dream," she said, almost defensively.

David Moroka flung to his feet, viper fast, and dashed toward Homer Crawford, his hands extended.

Automatically, Cliff Jackson stuck forward a foot in an attempt to trip him—and missed.

The South African, moving with blurring speed, grasped the unsuspecting Crawford by the right hand and arm, swung with fantastic speed and sent the American sprawling to the far side of the tent.

Homer Crawford, old in rough and tumble, was already rolling out. Before the inertia of his fall had given way, his right hand, only a split second before in the grip of the other, was fumbling for the 9 mm Noiseless holstered at his belt.

Rex Donaldson, a small handgun magically in his hand, was standing, half crouched on his thin, bent legs. The two brothers from Trinidad hadn't moved, their eyes bugging.

Moroka was spinning with the momentum of the sudden attack he'd made on his new chief. Now there was a gun in his own hand and he was darting for the tent opening.

Cliff yelled indignantly, "Stop him!"

Isobel, on her feet by now, both hands to her mouth, was staring at the goatskin tent covering, against which, a moment earlier, Crawford had been gently leaning his back as he talked.

There was a vicious slash in the leather and even as she pointed, the razor-sharp arm dagger's blade disappeared. There was the sound of running feet outside the tent.

Homer Crawford had assimilated the situation before the rest. He, too, was darting for the tent entrance, only feet behind Moroka.

Donaldson followed, muttering bitterly under his breath, his face twisted more as though in distaste than in fighting anger.

Cliff, too, finally saw light and dashed after the others, leaving only Isobel and the Peters brothers. They heard the muffled coughing of a silenced gun, twice, thrice and then half a dozen times, blurting together in automatic fire.

Homer Crawford shuffled through the sand on an awkward run, rounding the tent, weapon in hand.

There was a native on the ground making final spasmatic muscular movements in his death throes, and not more than three feet from him, coolly, David Moroka sat, bracing his elbows on his knees and aiming, two-handed, as his gun emptied itself.

Crawford brought his own gun up, seeking the target, and clipping at the same time, "We want him alive—"

It was too late. Two hundred feet beyond, a running tribesman, long arm dagger still in hand, stumbled, ran another three or four feet with hesitant steps, and then collapsed.

Moroka said, "Too late, Crawford. He would have got away." The South African started to his feet, brushing sand from his khaki bush shorts.

The others were beginning to come up and from the Tuareg encampment a rush of Guémama's men started in their direction.

Crawford said unhappily, looking down at the dead native at their feet, "I hate to see unnecessary killing."

Moroka looked at him questioningly. "Unnecessary? Another split second and his knife would have been in your gizzard. What do you want to give him, another chance?"

Crawford said uncomfortably, "Thanks, Dave, anyway. That was quick thinking."

"Thank God," Donaldson said, coming up, his wrinkled face scowling unhappily, first at the dead man at their feet, and then at the one almost a hundred yards away. "Are these local men? Where were your bodyguards?"

Cliff Jackson skidded to a halt, after rounding the tent. He'd heard only the last words. "What bodyguards?" he said.

Moroka looked at Crawford accusingly. "El Hassan," he said.

"Leader of all North Africa. And you haven't even got around to bodyguards? Do you fellows think you're playing children's games? Gentlemen, I assure you, the chips are down."

VI

El Hassan's Tuaregs were on the move. After half a century and more of relative peace the Apaches of the Sahara, the Sons of Shaitan and the Forgotten of Allah were again disappearing into the ergs to emerge here, there, and ghostlike to disappear again. They faded in and faded away again, and even in their absence dominated all.

El Hassan was on the move, as all men by now knew, and he, who was not for the amalgamation of all North Africa, was judged against him. And who, in the Sahara, could afford to be against El Hassan when his Tuaregs were everywhere?

Refugees poured into Tamanrasset for the security of Arab Legion arms, or into In Salah and Reggan to the north, or Agades and Zinder to the south. Refugees who had already taken their stand with the Arab Union and Pan-Islam. Refugees who were men of property and would know more of this El Hassan before risking their wealth. Refugees who took no stand, but dreaded those who drank the milk of war, no matter the cause for which they fought. Refugees who fled simply because others fled, for terror is a most contagious disease.

Colonel Midan Ibrahim of the crack motorized units of the Arab Legion which occupied Tamanrasset, was fuming. His task was a double one. First, to hold Tamanrasset and its former French stronghold Fort Laperrine; second, to keep open his lines of communication with Ghadmès and Ghat, in Arab Union dominated Libya. To hold them until further steps were decided upon by his superiors in Cairo and the Near East—whatever these steps might be. Colonel Midan Ibrahim was too low in the Arab Union hierarchy to be in on such privy matters.

His original efforts, in pushing across the Sahara from Ghadmès and Ghat, had been no more than desert maneuvers. There had been no force other than nature's to say him nay. The Re-united Nations was an organization composed possibly of great powers, but in supposedly acting in unison they became a shrieking set of hair-tearing women; the whole being less than any of its individual parts. And El Hassan? No more than a rumor. In fact, an asset because this supposed mystery man of the desert, bent on uniting all North Africa under his domination, gave the Arab Union, its alibi for stepping in with Colonel Ibrahim's men.

Yes, the original efforts had been but a drill. But now his Arab Legion troopers were beginning to face reality. The supply trucks, coming down under convoy from Ghadmès, reported the water source at Ohanet destroyed. The major well would take a week or more to repair. Who had committed the sabotage? Some said the Tuareg, some said local followers of El Hassan, others, desert tribesmen resentful of both the Arab Union and El Hassan.

One of his routine patrols, feeling out toward Meniet to the north, had suddenly dropped radio communication, almost in mid-sentence. A relieving patrol had thus far found nothing, the armored car's tracks covered over by the sands.

And rumors, rumors, rumors, Colonel Midan Ibrahim, born of aristocratic Alexandrian blood, though trained to a sharp edge in Near Eastern warfare, was basically city bred. The gloss of desert training might take on him, but the bedouin life itself was not in his experience, and it was hard for him to trace the dividing line between possibility and fantasy.

Rumors, rumors, rumors. They seemed capable of sweeping from one end of the Sahara to the other in a matter of hours. Faster, it would seem than the information could be dispensed by radio. El Hassan was here. El Hassan was there. El Hassan was marching on Rabat, in Morocco; El Hassan had just signed a treaty with the Soviet Complex; El Hassan had been assassinated by a disgruntled follower. Or El Hassan was a renegade Christian; El Hassan was a Moslem of Sheriffian blood, a direct descendant of the Prophet; El Hassan was a pagan come up from Dahomey and practiced ritual cannibalism; El Hassan was a Jew, a veteran of the Israel debacle.

But this Colonel Ibrahim knew—the Tuareg had gone over to the new movement en masse. Something there was in El Hassan and his dream that had appealed to the Forgotten of Allah. The Tuareg, for the first time since the French Camel Corps had broken their strength, were united—united and on the move.

The Tuareg were everywhere. In most sinister fashion—everywhere. And all were El Hassan's men.

Colonel Ibrahim fumed and wondered what kept his superiors from sending in additional columns, additional armored elements. And, above all, adequate air cover. Ha! Give the colonel sufficient aircraft and he'd begin snuffing out bedouin life like candles—and bring the Peace of Allah to the Ahaggar.

So Colonel Ibrahim fumed, demanded further orders from mum superiors, and put his legionnaires to work on bigger and better gun emplacements, trenches and pillboxes surrounding Fort Laperinne and Tamanrasset.

El Hassan's personal entourage numbered exactly twenty persons. Of these, five were his immediate English-speaking, Western-educated supporters, Cliff, Isobel and the new Jack and Jimmy Peters and Dave Moroka. Rex Donaldson had been sent south again to operate in Senegal and Mali, to take over direction of the rapidly spreading movement in such centers as Bamako and Mopti and later, if possible, in Dakar.

The other fifteen were carefully selected Tuareg, picked from among Guémama's tribesmen taking care to show no preference to any tribe or clan, and taking particular care to choose men who fought coolly, unexcitedly, and didn't froth at the mouth when in action; men who were slow to charge wildly into the enemy's guns—but slower still to retreat when the going was hot. El Hassan was prone to neither hero nor coward in his personal body-guard.

They kept under movement. In Abelessa one day, almost in range of the mobile artillery of the Arab Legion; in Timassao the next, checking the wells that meant everything to a desert force; the following day as far south as the Tamesna region to rally the less warlike Irreguenaten, a half-breed Tuareg people largely held in scorn by those of the Ahaggar.

Homer Crawford was killing time whilst stirring up as much noise and dust as his handful of followers could manage. Killing time until Elmer Allen from the Chaambra country, Bey-ag-Ak-hamouk from the Teda, and Kenny Ballalou from the west could show up with their columns. He had no illusions of how things now stood. At best, he could hold together a thousand Tuareg fighting men. No more. The economics of desert life prevented him a larger force, unless he had the resources of the modern world at hand, and he didn't. Besides that, the Tuareg confederation could provide no larger number of fighting men and at the same time continue their desert economy.

He stood now with Isobel, Cliff and Dave Moroka in one of the western type tents which the Peters brothers had brought with them in their hover-lorries, and poured over the half-adequate maps which covered the area.

Dave Moroka traced with a finger. "If we could dominate these wells running to Djanet, our Arab Union friends would have only their one line of supply going through Temassinine to Ghademès. That's a long haul, Homer."

Homer Crawford scowled thoughtfully. "That involves only four wells. If Ibrahim's legionnaires staked out only three armored vehicles at each water hole, they could hold them. Our camelmen could never take armor."

Moroka frowned, too. "We've got to start some sort of action, or the men will start dribbling away."

Cliff Jackson said, "Bey and Kenny and Elmer should be coming soon. I heard a radio item this morning about a big pro-El Hassan movement starting in the Sudan among the Teda."

Moroka said, "We need some sort of quick, spectacular victory. The bedouin can lose interest as quickly as they can get steamed up, and thus far we haven't given them anything but words—promises."

"You're right," Homer growled, "but there's nothing we can do right now but mark time. Irritate the Arabs a bit. Keep them from spreading out."

Isobel brought coffee, handing around the small Moroccan cups. She said, "Well, one thing is certain. We get supplies soon or start eating jerked goat and camel milk curds."

Moroka said in irritation, "It's not funny."

Isobel raised her eyebrows. "I didn't mean it to be. Have you ever been on a camel curd diet?"

"Yes, I have," Moroka said impatiently. He turned back to Homer Crawford. "How about waylaying an armored car or so, just in the way of giving the men something exciting to do?"

Crawford ran a hand back through his short hair. "Confound it, Dave, can you picture what a Recoilless-Brenn gun would do to a harka of our charging camelmen? We can't let these people be butchered."

"I wasn't thinking of wild charges," Moroka argued.

They had both turned away from Isobel, in their discussion. Now she looked at them, strangely. And especially at Homer Crawford. His brusqueness toward her didn't seem the old Homer.

There was a bustle from outside and a guardsman stuck his head in the tent entrance and reported in Tamaheq that a small camel patrol approached.

The four of them went out. Coming up were a dozen Tuareg and two motor vehicles.

Cliff said, "Something new."

Moroka said, "We can use the transport."

"Let's see who they are, before we start requisitioning their property," Homer said dryly.

The two desert trucks had hardly come to a halt before the camouflaged tents and hover-lorries of El Hassan's small encampment before a heavy-set, gray haired Negro, whose energy belied his weight, bounced down from the seat adjacent to the driver's in the lead vehicle and stomped belligerently to the group before the tent.

"What is the meaning of this?" he snapped.

Homer Crawford looked at him. "I'm sure I don't know as yet, Dr. Smythe. Neither you nor these followers of mine have informed me as to what has transpired. Won't you enter my quarters here and we'll go into it under more comfortable conditions?" He glanced upward at the midday Saharan sun.

The other seemed taken aback at Crawford calling him by name. He squinted at the man who was seemingly his captor.

"Crawford!" he snapped. "Dr. Homer Crawford! See here, what is the meaning of this?"

Homer said, "Dr. Warren Harding Smythe, may I present Isobel Cunningham, Clifford Jackson and David Moroka, of my staff?"

"Huuump. I met Miss Cunningham and, I believe, Mr. Jackson at that ridiculous meeting in Timbuktu, a short time ago." The doctor peered over his glasses at Moroka.

The wiry South African nodded his head. "A pleasure, Doctor." He held open the tent entrance.

Smythe snorted again and stomped inside to escape the sun's glare.

In the shade of the tent's interior, Isobel clucked at him and hurried to get a drink of water from a moist water cooler. Homer Crawford motioned the other to a seat, and took one himself. "Now then, Dr. Smythe."

The indignant medic blurted, "Those confounded bandits out there—"

"Irregular camel cavalry," Crawford amended gently.

"They've kidnapped me and my staff. I demand that you intercede, if you have any influence with them."

"What were you doing?" Crawford was frowning at the other. Actually, he had no idea of the circumstances under which the probably overenthusiastic Tuareg troopers had rounded up the American medical man.

"Doing? You know perfectly well I represent the American Medical Relief. My team has been in the vicinity of Silet, working with the nomads. The country is rife with everything from rickets to syphilis! Eighty per cent of these people suffer from trachoma. My team—"

"Just a moment," Moroka said. "You mean out in those two trucks you have a complete American medical setup? Assistants and all?"

Smythe said stiffly, "I have two American nurses with me and four Algerians recruited in Oran. This sort of interference with my work is insufferable and—"

The South African was staring at Homer Crawford.

Cliff Jackson cleared his throat. "It seems as though El Hassan has just acquired a Department of Health."

"El Hassan?" Smythe stuttered. "What, what?"

Isobel said softly, "Dr. Smythe, surely you have heard of El Hassan."

"Heard of him? I've heard of nothing else for the past month! Confounded ignorant barbarian. What this part of the world needs is less intertribal, interracial, international fighting, not more. The man's a raving lunatic and—"

Isobel said gently, "Doctor . . . may I introduce you to El Hassan?"

"What . . . what—?" For the briefest of moments, there was an element of timorness in the sputtering doctor's voice. Then suddenly he comprehended.

He pointed at Homer Crawford accusingly. "You're El Hassan!"

Homer nodded, seriously, "That's correct, Doctor."

The doctor's eyes went around the four of them. "You've done what you were driving at there at that meeting in Timbuktu. You're trying to unite these people in spite of themselves and then drag them, willy-nilly, into the twentieth century."

Homer still nodded.

Smythe shook an indignant finger at him. "I told you then, Crawford, and I tell you now. These natives are not suited for such sudden change. Already they are subject to mass neurosis because they cannot adjust to a world that changes too quickly."

"I wonder if that doesn't apply to the rest of us as well," Cliff said unhappily. "But the changes go on, if we like them or not. Can you think of any way to turn them off?"

The doctor snorted.

Homer Crawford said, "Dr. Smythe, the die is already cast. The question now becomes, will you join us?"

"Join you! Certainly not!"

Crawford said evenly, "Then I might suggest that, first, you will not be allowed to operate in my territory." He considered for a moment, grinning inwardly, but on the surface his expression serene. He added, "And second, that you will probably have difficulties procuring an exit visa from my domains."

"Exit visa! Are you jesting? See here, my good man, you realize I am a citizen of the United States of the Americas and—"

"A country," Homer yawned, "with which I have not as yet opened diplomatic relations, and hence has little representation in North Africa."

The doctor was bug-eying him. He began sputtering again. "This isn't funny. You're an American citizen yourself. And you, Miss Cunningham and—"

Isobel said sadly, "As a matter of fact, the last we heard, the State Department representative told us our passports were invalid."

Crawford leaned forward. "Look here, Doctor. You don't see eye to eye with us on matters socio-economic. However, as a medical man, I submit that joining my group . . . ah, that is, until you can secure an exit visa from my authorities . . . will give you an excellent opportunity to practice your science here in the Sahara under the wing of El Hassan. I'll assign a place for your trucks and tents. Please consider the question and let me have your answer at your leisure. Meanwhile, we will prepare a desert feast suitable to the high esteem in which we hold you."

They looked after the doctor, as he left, and Moroka chuckled. However, Isobel was watching Homer Crawford quizzically.

She said finally, "We rode over him a little in the roughshod manner, didn't we?"

Homer Crawford growled uncomfortably, "Particularly when we finally have our showdown with the Arab Legion, a medic will be priceless."

Isobel said softly, "And the end justifies the means—"

Homer shot a quick, impatient look at her. "The good doctor and his people are in the Sahara to work with the Tuareg and the Teda and the rest of the bedouin. Beyond that, he has the same dream we have—of developing this continent of our racial background."

"But he doesn't believe in your methods, Homer, and we're forcing him to follow El Hassan's road in spite of his beliefs."

Moroka had been peering at the two of them narrowly. "You don't make omelets without breaking eggs," he said, his voice on the overbearing side.

She spun on him. "But the omelets don't turn out so well if some of the eggs you use are rotten."

The South African's voice turned gentle. "Miss Cunningham," he said, "working in the field, like this, can have its rugged side for a young and delicate woman—"

"Delicate!" she snapped. "I'll have you know—"

"Hey, everybody, hold it," Cliff injected. "What goes on?"

Dave Moroka shrugged. "It just seems to me that Isobel might do better back in Dakar, or in New York with your friend Jake Armstrong. Somewhere where her sensibilities wouldn't be so bruised, and where her assets"—his eyes went up and down her lithe body—"could be put to better use."

Isobel's sepia face had gone a shade or more lighter. She said, very flatly, "My assets, Mr. Moroka, are in my head."

Homer Crawford said disgustedly, "O.K., O.K., let's all knock it off."

His eyes flicked back and forth between them, in definite command. "I don't want to hear any more in the way of personalities between you two."

Moroka shrugged again. "Yes, sir," he said without inflection.

Isobel turned away and took up some paperwork, without further words. She suppressed her feeling of seething indignation.

Homer Crawford, under his pressures, was changing. Possibly, she had told herself before, it was change for the better. The need was for a strong man, perhaps even a ruthless one.

The Homer Crawford she had first known was an easier going

man than he who had snapped an abrupt order to her a moment ago. The Homer she had first known requested things of his teammates and friends. El Hassan had learned to command.

The Homer she had first known could never have ridden, roughshod, over the basically gentle Dr. Smythe.

The Homer she had first known, when the El Hassan scheme was still aborning, had thought of himself as a member of a team. He was quick to ask advice of all, and quick to take it if it had validity. Now Homer, as El Hassan, was depending less and less upon the opinions of those surrounding him, more and more upon his own decisions which he seemed to sometimes reach purely through intuition.

The El Hassan dream was still upon her, but, womanlike, she wondered if she liked the would-be tyrant of all North Africa as well as she had once liked the easy-going American idealist, Homer Crawford.

Jack and Jimmy Peters, the brothers from Trinidad, entered, the former carrying a couple of books.

They'd evidently failed to note the raised voices and wore their customary serious expressions. Jack looked at Homer and said, "Cu vi scias Esperanton?"

Homer Crawford's eyebrows went up but he said, "Jes, mi parolas Esperanto tre bona, mi pensas."

"Bona," Jack said, "Tre bona."

"Jes, estas bele," his brother said.

Moroka was scowling back and forth from one of them to the other. "I thought I had a fairly good working knowledge of the world's more common languages," he said, "but that goes by me. It sounds like a cross between Italian and pig-Latin."

Homer said to the Peters brothers, "Let's drop Esperanto so that Dave, Isobel and Cliff can follow us. We can give it a whirl later, if you'd like, just for the practice."

Isobel said slowly, "Mi parolas Esperanto, malgranda." Then in English, "I took it for kicks while I was still in school. Kind of rusty now, though."

"Esperanto?" Cliff said. "You mean that gobblydygook so-called international language?"

Jack Peters looked at him, serious faced as always. "What is wrong with an international language, Mr. Jackson?"

Cliff was taken aback. "Search me. But it doesn't seem to have proved very practical. It didn't catch on."

"Well, more than you might think," Isobel told him. "There are probably hundreds of thousands of persons in one part of the world or another who can get along in Esperanto."

Moroka said impatiently, "What're a few hundred thousands of people in a world population like ours? Cliff's right. It never took hold."

Homer said, "All right, Jack and Jimmy. You boys evidently have something on your minds. Let everybody sit down and listen to it."

Even before they got thoroughly settled, Jack Peters was launching into his pitch.

"We need an official language," he said. "The El Hassan movement has set as a goal the uniting of all North Africa. We might start here in the Sahara, but it's just a start. Ultimately, the idea is to reach from Morocco to Egypt and from the Mediterranean to . . . to where? The Congo?"

"Actually, we've never set exact limits," Homer said.

"Ultimately all Africa," Dave Moroka muttered softly. He ignored the manner in which Isobel contemplated him from the side of her eyes.

"All right," the West Indian said. "There are more than seven hundred major languages, not counting dialects, in Africa. Sooner or later, we need an official language, what is it going to be?"

"Why one official language? Why not several?" Cliff scowled. "Say Arabic, here in this area. Swahili on the East coast. And, say, Songhoi along the Niger, and Wolof, the Senegalese lingua franca, and—"

"You see," Peters interrupted. "Already you have half a dozen and you haven't even got out of this immediate vicinity as yet. Let me develop my point."

Homer Crawford was becoming interested. "Go on, Jack," he said.

Jack Peters pointed a finger at him. "To be the hero-symbol we have in mind, El Hassan is going to have to be able to communicate with all of his people. He's not going to be able to speak Arabic to, say, a Masai in Kenya. They hate the Arabs. He's not going to be able to speak Swahili to a Moroccan, they've never heard of the language. He can't speak Tamaheq to the Imraguen, they're scared to death of the Tuareg."

Homer said thoughtfully, "A common language would be fine. It'd solve a lot of problems. But it doesn't seem to be in the cards. Why not adopt as our official language the one in which the most of our people will be able to communicate? Say, Arabic?"

Jack was shaking his head seriously. "And antagonize all the Arab hating Bantu in Africa? It's no go, Homer."

"Well, then, say French—or English."

"English is the most international language in the world," Moroka said. But his face was thoughtful, as those of the others were becoming.

The West Indian was beginning to make his points now. "No, any of the European languages are out. The white man has been repudiated. Adopting English, French, Spanish, Portuguese or Dutch, as our official language would antagonize whole sections of the continent."

"Why Esperanto?" Cliff scowled. "Why not, say, Nov-Esperanto, or Ido, or Interlingua?"

Jimmy Peters put in a word now. "Actually, any one of them would possibly do, but we have a head start with Esperanto. Some years ago both Jack and I became avid Esperantists, being naïve enough in those days to think an international language would ultimately solve all man's problems. And both Homer and Isobel seem to have a working knowledge of the language."

Homer said, "So have the other members of my former Re-united Nations team. That's where those books you found came from. Elmer, Bey, Kenny . . . and Abe . . . and I used to play around with it when we were out in the desert, just to kill time. We also used it as sort of a secret language when we wanted to communicate and didn't know if those around us might understand some English."

"I still don't get the picture," Cliff argued. "If we picked the most common half a dozen languages in the territory we cover, then millions of these people wouldn't have to study a second language. But if you adapt Esperanto as an official language then everybody is going to have to learn something new. And that's not going to be easy for our ninety-five per cent illiterate followers."

Isobel said thoughtfully, "Well, it's a darn sight easier to learn Esperanto than any other language we decided to make official."

"Why?" Cliff said argumentatively.

Jack Peters took over. "Because it's almost unbelievably easy to learn. English, by the way, is extremely difficult. For instance, spelling and pronunciation are absolutely phonetic in Esperanto and there are only five vowel sounds where most national languages have twenty or so. And each sound in the alphabet has one sound only and any sound is always rendered by the same letter."

Dave Moroka said, "Actually, I don't know anything at all about this Esperanto."

The West Indian took him in, with a dominating glance. "Take grammar and syntax which can take up volumes in other languages. Esperanto has exactly sixteen short rules. And take vocabularies. For instance, in English we often form the feminine of a noun by adding ess—actor-actress, tiger-tigress. But not always. We don't say bull-bulless or ghost-ghostess. In Esperanto you simply add the feminine ending to any noun—there's no exception to any rule."

Jack Peters was caught up in his subject. "Still comparing it to English, realize that spelling and pronunciation in English are highly irregular and one letter can have several different sounds, and one sound may be represented by different letters. And there are even silent letters which are written but not pronounced like the ugh in though. There are none of these irregularities in Esperanto. And the sounds are all sharp with none of such subtle differences as, say, bed/bad/bard/bawd, that sort of thing."

Jimmy Peters said, "The big item is that any averagely intelligent person can begin speaking Esperanto within a few hours. Within a week of even moderate study, say three or four hours a day, he's astonishingly fluent."

Isobel said thoughtfully, "There'd be international advantages. It's always been a galling factor in Africans dealing with Europeans that they had to learn the European language involved. You couldn't expect your white man to learn kitchen kaffir, or Swahili, or whatever, not when you got on the diplomatic level."

Cliff Jackson was thinking out loud. "So far, El Hassan is an unknown. Rumor has it that he's everything from a renegade Egyptian, to an escaped Mau-Mau chief, to a Senegalese sergeant formerly in the French West African forces. But when he starts running into the press and they find that Homer and his closest associates all speak English, and most of them with an American accent, there's going to be some fat in the fire."

"And El Hassan will have lost some of his mysterious glamour," Homer added thoughtfully.

Even Moroka, the South African, was beginning to accept the idea. "If El Hassan, himself, refused in the presence of foreigners ever to speak anything but Esperanto, the aura of mystery would continue."

Jimmy Peters, elaborating and obviously pushing an opinion he and his brother had already discussed, said, "We make it a rule that every school, both locally taught and foreign, must teach Esperanto as a required subject. All El Hassan governmental affairs would be conducted in that language. Anybody at all trying to get anywhere in the new regime would have to learn the official inter-African tongue."

"Oh, brother," Cliff groaned, "that means me." He brightened. "We haven't any books or anything, as yet."

Isobel laughed at him. "I'll take on your studies, Cliff. We have a few books. Those that Homer and his team used to kill time with. And as soon as we're in a position to make requests for foreign aid of the great powers, Esperanto grammars, dictionaries and so forth can be high on the list."

With a sharp cry, almost a bark, a figure jumped into the entrance and with a bound into the center of the tent, submachinegun in hand. "All right, everybody. On your feet. The place is raided!"

Dave Moroka leaped to his feet, his hand tearing with blurring speed for his holstered hand gun. "Where's that bodyguard?" he yelled.

VII

"Hold it," Homer Crawford roared, jumping to his own feet and grabbing the South African in his arms. He glared at the newcomer. "Kenny, you idiot, you're lucky you don't have a couple of holes in you."

Kenny Ballalou, grinning widely, stared at Dave Moroka. "Jeepers," he said, "you got that gun out fast. Don't you ever stick 'em up when somebody has the drop on you?"

Dave Moroka relaxed, the side arm dropping back into its holster. Homer Crawford released him and the South African ran a hand over his mouth and shook his head ruefully at Kenny.

Isobel and Cliff crowded up, the one to kiss Kenny happily, the other to pound him on the back.

Homer made introductions to Dave Moroka and the Peters brothers.

"I've told you about Kenny," he wound it up. "I sent him over to the west to raise a harka of Nemadi to help in taking Tamanrasset." He joined Cliff Jackson in giving the smaller man an affectionate blow on the shoulder. "What luck did you have, Kenny?"

Kenny Ballalou rubbed himself ruefully. "If you two will stop beating, I'll tell you. I didn't recruit a single Nemadi."

Homer Crawford looked at him.

Kenny said to the tent at large. "Anybody got a drink around here? Good grief, have I been covering ground."

Isobel bustled off to a corner where she'd amassed most of their remaining European type supplies, but she kept her attention on him.

Dave Moroka said, his voice unbelieving, "You mean you haven't brought any assistance at all?"

Kenny grinned around at them. "I didn't say that. I said I didn't recruit any of the Nemadi. I never even got as far as their territory."

Homer Crawford sank back onto the small crate he'd been using as a chair before Kenny's precipitate entrance. "O.K.," he said, "stop dramatizing and let us know what happened."

Kenny spread his hands in a sweeping gesture. "The country's alive from here to Bidon Cinq and south to the Niger. Bourem and Gao have gone over to El Hassan and a column of followers was descending on Niamey. They should be there by now. I never got as far as Nemadi country. I could have recruited ten thousand fighting men, but I didn't know what we'd do with them in this country. So I weeded through everybody who volunteered and took only veterans. Men who'd formerly been in the French forces, or British, or whatever. Louis Wallington and his team were in Bourem when I got there and—"

"Who is Louis Wallington?" Jack Peters said.

Homer looked over at the Peters brothers and Dave Moroka. "Head of a six-man Sahara Development Project team like the one I used to head." His eyes went back to Kenny. "What about Louis?"

"He's come in with us. Didn't know how to get in touch, so he was working on his own. And Pierre Dupaine. Remember him, the fellow from Guadeloupe in the French West Indies, used to be an operative of the African Affairs sector of the French Community? Well, he and a half dozen of his colleagues have come in and were leading an expedition on Timbuktu. But Timbuktu had already joined up too, before they got there—"

"Wow," Homer said. "It's really spreading."

Cliff said, "Why isn't all this on the radio?"

Isobel had brought Kenny a couple of ounces of cognac from their meager supply. He knocked it back thankfully.

Kenny said to Cliff, "Things are moving too fast, and communications have gone to pot." He looked at Homer. "Have any of these journalists found you yet?"

"What journalists?"

Kenny laughed. "You'll find out. Half the newspapers, magazines, newsreels and TV outfits in the world are sending every man they can release into this area. They're going batty trying to find El Hassan. Man, do you realize the extent of the country your followers now dominate?"

Homer said blankly, "I hadn't thought of it. Besides, most of what you've been saying is news to us here. We've been keeping on the prod."

Kenny grinned widely. "Well, the nearest I can figure it, El Hassan is ruler of an area about the size of Mexico. At least it was yesterday. By today, you can probably tack on Texas."

Jimmy Peters, serious faced as usual, said, "Things are moving so fast, we're going to have to run to keep ahead of El Hassan's followers. One thing, Homer, we're going to have to have a press secretary."

"Elmer Allen was going to handle that, but he's still up north," Isobel said.

"I'll do it. Used to be a newspaperman, when I was younger," Dave Moroka said quickly.

Isobel frowned and began to say something, but Homer said, "Great, you handle that, Dave." Then to Kenny, "Where're your men and how well are they armed?"

"Well, that's one trouble," Kenny said unhappily. "We requisitioned motor transport from some of the Sahara Afforestation Project oases down around Tessalit. In fact, Ralph Sandell, their chief mucky-muck in those parts, has come over to us. But we haven't got much in the way of shooting irons."

Homer Crawford closed his eyes wearily. "What it boils down to, still, is that a hundred of those Arab Legionnaires, with their armor, could finish us all off in ten minutes if it came to open battle."

El Hassan continued moving his headquarters, usually daily, but he eluded the journalists only another twelve hours. Then they were upon the mobile camp like locusts.

And David Moroka took over with a calm efficiency that impressed all. In the first place, he explained, El Hassan was much too busy to handle the press except for one conference a week. In the second place, he spoke only Esperanto to foreigners. Meanwhile, he, Dave Moroka, would handle all their questions, make arrangements for suitable photographs, and for the TV and newsreel boys to trundle their equipment as near the front lines as possible. And, meanwhile, James and John Peters of El Hassan's staff had prepared press releases covering the El Hassan movement and its program.

Homer, to the extent possible, was isolated from the new elements descending upon his encampment. Attempting anything else would have been out of the question. At this point, he was getting approximately four hours of sleep a night.

Kenny Ballalou was continually coming and going in a mad attempt to handle the logistics of supplying several thousand men in a desert area all but devoid of either water or graze, not to speak of food, petroleum products and ammunition.

Isobel and Cliff were thrown into the positions of combination secretaries, ministers of finance, assistant bodyguards, and all else that nobody else seemed to handle, including making coffee.

It was Isobel who approached a subject which had long worried her, as they drove across country, the only occupants of one of the original hover-lorries, during a camp move.

She said, hesitantly, "Homer, is it a good idea to give Dave such a free hand with the press? You know, there are some fifty or so of them around now and they must be influencing the TV, radio, magazines and newspapers of the world."

"He seems to know more about it than any of the rest of us," Homer said, his eyes on the all but sand-obliterated way. "We're going to have to move more of the men south. We simply haven't got water enough for them. There'd be enough in Tamanrasset, but not out here. Make a note to cover this with Kenny. I wonder where Bey is, and Elmer."

Isobel made a note. She said, "Yes, but the trouble is, he's a comparative newcomer. Are you sure he's in complete accord with the original plan, Homer? Does the El Hassan dream mean the same to him as it does to you, and . . . well, me?"

He shot her an impatient glance, even as he hit the lift lever to raise them over a small dune. "You and Dave don't hit it off very well. He's a good man, so far as I can see."

Her delicate forehead wrinkled and her pixie face showed puzzlement. "I don't know why. I get along with most people, Homer."

He patted her hand. "You can't please everybody, Isobel. Listen, something's got to be done about this king-size mob of camp followers we've got. Did you know Common Europe sent in a delegation this morning?"

"Delegation? Common Europe—?"

"Yeah. Haven't had time to discuss it with you. They found us just before we raised camp. Evidently, the British Commonwealth and possibly the Soviet Complex—some Chinese, I think—are also trying to locate us. Half of these people are without their own equipment and supplies, but that's not what worries me right now. We used to be able to camouflage our headquarters camp. Dig into the desert and avoid the aircraft. But if a group of bungling Common Market diplomats can locate us, what's to keep the Arab Legion from doing it and blessing us with a stick of neopalm bombs?"

Isobel said, "Look, before we leave Dave. Did you know he was confiscating all radio equipment brought into our camp by the newsmen and whoever else?"

Homer frowned. "Well, why?"

"Espionage, Dave says. He's afraid some of these characters might be in with the Arab Union and inform on us."

"Well, that makes some sense," Homer nodded.

"Does it?" Isobel grumbled.

He shot an irritated glance at her again and said impatiently, "Can't the poor guy do anything right?"

"My woman's intuition is working," Isobel grumbled.

Dave Moroka came into headquarters tent without introduction. He was one of the half dozen who had permission for this. He had a sheaf of papers in his left hand and was frowning unhappily.

"What's the crisis?" Homer said.

"Scouts coming up say your pal Bey-ag-Akhamouk is on the way. Evidently, with a big harka of Teda from the Sudan."

"Great." Homer crowed. "Now we'll get going."

"Ha!" Dave said. "From what we hear, a good many are camel mounted. How are we going to feed them? Already some of the Songhai Kenny brought up from the south have drifted away, unhappy about supplies."

"Bey's a top man," Homer told him. "The best. He'll have some ideas on our tactics. Meanwhile, we can turn over most of his men to one of the new recruits, and head them down to take Fort Lamy. With Fort Lamy and Lake Chad in our hands we'll control a chunk of Africa so big everybody else will start wondering why they shouldn't jump on the bandwagon while the going is good."

Dave said, "Well, that brings up something else, Homer. These new recruits. In the past couple of days, forty or fifty men who used to be connected with African programs sponsored by everybody from the Reunited Nations to this gobblydygook outfit Cliff and Isobel once worked for, the AFAA, have come over to El Hassan. The number will probably double by tomorrow, and triple the next day."

"Fine," Homer said. "What's wrong with that? These are the people that will really count in the long run."

"Nothing's wrong with it, within reason. But we're going to

have to start becoming selective, Homer. We've got to watch what jobs we let these people have, how much responsibility we give them."

Homer Crawford was frowning at him. "How do you mean?"

"See here," the wiry South African said plaintively, "when El Hassan started off there were only a half dozen or so who had the dream, as you call it. O.K. You could trust any one of them. Bey, Kenny, Elmer, Cliff, this Jake Armstrong that you've sent to New York, Rex Donaldson, then Jimmy and Jack Peters and myself. We all came in when the going was rough, if not impossible. But now things are different. It looks as though El Hassan might actually win."

"So?" Homer didn't get it.

"So from now on, you're going to have an infiltration of cloak and dagger lads from every outfit with an interest in North Africa. Potential traitors, potential assassins, subversives and what not."

Homer was scowling at him. "Confound it, what do you suggest? That these Johnny-Come-Latelies be second-class citizens?"

"Not exactly that, but this isn't funny. We've got to screen them. The trouble with this movement is that it's a one-man deal, and has to be. The average African is either a barbarian or an actual savage, one ethnic degree lower. He wants a hero-symbol to follow. O.K., you're it. But remember both Moctezuma and Atahualpa. Their socio-economic systems pyramided up to them. The Spanish conquistadores, being old hands at sophisticated European-type intrigue, quickly sized up the situation. They kidnaped the hero-symbol, the big cheese, and later killed him. And the Inca and the Aztec cultures collapsed."

Homer was scowling at him unhappily.

Dave summed it up. "All we need is one fuzzy minded commie from the Soviet Complex, or one super-dooper democrat who thinks that El Hassan stands in the way of freedom, whatever that is, and bingo a couple of bullets in your tummy and the El Hassan movement folds its tents like the Arabs and takes a powder, as the old expression goes."

"You have your point," Homer Crawford admitted. "Follow through, Dave. Figure out some screening program."

Cliff came in. "Hey, Homer. Guess what old Jake has done."

"Jake Armstrong?"

"He's swung the Africa for Africans Association in New York

over to us. They've raised a million bucks. What'll we do with it? How can he get anything to us?"

"We'll have him plow it back into publicity and further fund raising campaigns," Homer said. "That's the way it's done. You raise some money for some cause and then spend it all on a bigger campaign to raise still more money, and what you get from that one you plow into a still bigger campaign."

Cliff said, "Don't you ever get anything out of it?"

Dave and Homer both laughed.

Cliff said, "I've got some still better news."

"Good news, we can use," Homer said.

The big Californian looked at him in pretended awe. "A poet no less," he said.

"Shut up," Homer said. "What's the news?"

The fact of the matter was, he was becoming increasingly impatient of the continual banter expected of him by Cliff and even the others. As original members of the team, they expected an intimacy that he was finding it increasingly difficult to deliver. Among other things, he wished that Cliff, in particular, would mind his attitude when such followers as Guémama were present. The El Hassan posture could be maintained only in never to be compromised dignity.

Bey had once compared him to Alexander, to Homer's amusement at the time. But now he was beginning to sympathize with the position the Macedonian leader had found himself in, betwixt the King-God conscious Persians, and the rough and ready Companions who formed his bodyguard and crack cavalry units. A King-God simply didn't banter with his subordinates, not even his blood-kin.

Cliff scowled at him now, at the sharpness of Homer's words, but he made his report.

"Our old pal, Sven Zetterberg. He's gone out on a limb. Because of the great danger of this so-far localized fight spreading into world-wide conflict—says old Sven—the Reunited Nations will not tolerate the combat going into the air. He says that if either El Hassan or the Arab Legion resort to use of aircraft, the Reunited Nations will send in its air fleet."

"Wow," Homer said. "All the aircraft we've got are a few slow-moving heliocopters that Kenny brought up with him."

Dave Moroka snapped his fingers in a gesture of elation.

"That means Zetterberg is throwing his weight to our side."

Homer was on his feet. "Send for Kenny and Guémama and send a heliocopter down to pick up Bey and rush him here. He shouldn't be more than a day's march away. I wonder what Elmer is up to. No word at all from him. At any rate, we want an immediate council of war. With Arab Legion air cover eliminated, we can move in."

Cliff said sourly, "It's still largely rifles against armored cars, tanks, mobile artillery and even flame throwers."

All the old hands were present. They stood about a map table, Homer and Bey-ag-Akhamouk at one end, the rest clustered about. Isobel sat in a chair to the rear, stenographer's pad on her knees.

Bey was clipping out suggestions.

"We have them now. Already our better trained men are heading up for Temassinine to the north and Fort Charlet to the east. We'll lose men but we'll knock out every water hole between here and Libya. We'll cut every road, blow what few bridges there are."

Jack Peters said worriedly, "But the important thing is Tamanrasset. What good—"

"We're cutting their supply line," Bey told him. "Can't you see? Colonel Ibrahim and his motorized column will be isolated in Tamanrasset. They won't be able to get supplies through without an air lift and Sven Zetterberg's ultimatum kills that possibility. They're blocked off."

Jimmy Peters was as confused as his brother. "So what? to use the Americanism. They have both food and water in abundance. They can hold out indefinitely. Meanwhile, our forces are undisciplined irregulars. We gain a thousand recruits a day. They come galloping in on camel-back or in beat-up old vehicles, firing their hunting rifles into the air. But we also lose a thousand a day. They get bored, or hungry, and decide to go back to their flocks, or their jobs on the new Sahara projects. At any rate, they drift off again. It looks to me that, if Colonel Ibrahim can hold out another week or so, our forces might melt away—all except the couple of hundred or so European and American educated followers. And, cut down to that number, they'll eliminate us in no time flat."

Homer Crawford was eying him in humor. "You're no fighting man, Peters. Tell me, what is the single most fearsome enemy of an ultra-mechanized soldier with the latest in military equipment and super-firepower weapons?"

Jimmy Peters was blank. "I suppose a similarly armed opponent."

Homer smiled at him. "Rather, a man with a knife."

The expressions of the Peters brothers showed resentment. "We weren't jesting."

"Neither was I," Homer rapped. He looked around at the rest, including Bey and Kenny. "What happens to a modern mechanized army when it runs out of gasoline? What happens to a water-cooled machine gun when there is no water? What use is a howitzer when the target is a single man in ten acres of cover? Gentlemen, have any of you ever studied the tactics of Abd-el-Krim or, more recently still, Tito? Bey, I assume you have."

He had their attention.

"During the Second War," Homer continued, "this Yugoslavian Tito tied up two Nazi army corps with a handful of partisans—guerrillas. The most modern army in the world, the German Panzers, tried to ferret him out for five years, and couldn't. There are other examples. The Chinese operating against the Japs in the same war. Or one of the classic examples is Abd-el-Krim destroying two different Spanish armies in the Moroccan Rif in the 1920s. His barefoot men, armed with rifles, took on Primo de Rivera's modernized Spanish armies and trounced them."

Bey said, "Homer's right. Our only tactics are guerrilla ones."

Homer Crawford looked at Guémama, who had been standing in the background, unfamiliar with the language these others spoke, but holding his dignity. Crawford said, diplomatically, "And what sayest thou, O chieftain of the Tuareg?"

Guémama was gratified at the attention. He said in Tamaheq, "As all men know, O El Hassan, we now outnumber by thrice the Arab giaours may they burn in Gehennum. Therefore, let us rush in and kill them all."

Bey shuddered.

Homer Crawford nodded seriously. "Ai, Guémama, that would be the valorous way of the Tuareg. But the heart of El Hassan forbids him to sacrifice the lives of his people. Consequently, we shall use the tactics of the desert jackal. Instruct those of your people who are most cunning, to infiltrate Tamanrasset in the night. Let them not carry arms for they may well be searched by the Arab meleccha."

The Tuareg chieftain was intrigued. "And what shall they do in Tamanrasset, El Hassan? Suddenly seize arms, one night, and rise up in wrath against the Arab dogs and kill them all?"

Homer was shaking his head. "They will address themselves to the Haratin serfs and spread to them the message of El Hassan. They will be told that in the world of El Hassan each man shall be free to seek his own destiny to the extent his mind and abilities allow. And no man shall be the less because he was born a serf, and no man the more because he was born to wealth or power in the old days."

"Aiii," Guémama all but moaned. "But such a message—"

"Is the message of El Hassan, as all men know," Homer Crawford said flatly. He turned to Kenny Ballalou. "Kenny, take over this angle. We want as many propagandists in that town as possible. It's already choked with refugees, most of them not knowing what they're fleeing. We might get recruits there, too. But mostly we want to appeal to the sedentary natives in town. They've got to get the dreams, too. Promise them schools, land . . . I don't have to tell you."

"Right," Kenny said.

Isobel said, "Maybe I ought to get in on this, too. The women might do a better job than men on this slant. It's going to take a lot to get a Tuareg bedouin to sink to talking to a Haratin on an equal basis."

Bey and Homer had bent back over the maps, but before they could get back into the details of guerrilla warfare against Colonel Ibrahim and his legionnaires, they were halted by a controversy from without.

"What now?" Homer growled. "This camp is getting to be like a three-ring circus."

The entrance flap was pushed aside and three of Bey's Sudanese tribesmen half escorted, half pushed a newcomer front and center.

It was Fredric Ostrander, natty as usual, but now in khaki desert wear. He was obviously in a rage at the three rifle-carrying nomads who had him in charge.

Bey spoke to the Teda warriors in their own tongue. Then to Homer in Tamaheq, which he assumed the C.I.A. man didn't know, "They picked him up in the desert in a hover-jeep. He was evidently looking for our camp." He dismissed the three bedouin with a gesture.

Ostrander was outraged. He snapped at Homer Crawford, "I demand an explanation of this cavalier attack upon—"

His face expressionless, Homer held up a hand to quiet the smaller man. He looked at Jack Peters and raised his eyebrows. "Kion li la fremdul diras?"

Jack, serious as ever, replied in Esperanto, then turned to the American C.I.A. man and said, "El Hassan has requested that I translate for him. He speaks only the official language of North Africa to foreign representatives. Undoubtedly, sir, you have proper credentials?"

Had Fredric Ostrander been of lighter complexion, his color would have undoubtedly gone dark red.

"Look here, Crawford," he snapped. "I'm in no mood for nonsense. The State Department has sent me to your headquarters to make another attempt to bring some sense home to you. As an American citizen, owing alliance—"

Homer Crawford spoke in Esperanto to Jack Peters who nodded seriously and said to Ostrander, "El Hassan informs you he owes alliance only to the people of North Africa whose chosen leader he is."

Ostrander knew they were kidding him, but at the same time the stand being taken was actuality. He glared at the Americans present whom he knew, Bey, Isobel, Cliff and Kenny. He snapped, "Very well, but I repeat what I told you when last we met. The State Department of the United States of the Americas will not stand idly by and see this area taken over by elements dominated by red subversives."

"Holy Mackerel," Cliff growled, "are you still tooting that horn?"

Dave Moroka said sarcastically, "It's an old wheeze. The definition of a red subversive is anybody who doesn't see eye to eye with the United States. They've been pulling the gag for decades. Remember Guatemala and Cuba? Do anything that interferes with American business abroad and the cry goes up, he's an enemy of the free world!"

Ostrander spun on him, his eyes narrowing.

Dave laughed. "The definition of members of the free world,

of course, being anybody who follows the American line. Anybody is free, Spanish and Portuguese dictators, absolute monarchs in Arabia, Chinese warlords, if they're on the American side."

Ostrander snapped, "I don't believe we've met."

Moroka made a sweeping bow. "I'm afraid we don't move in the same circles. I've spent possibly a third of my life in prison—"

"Undoubtedly," Ostrander snorted.

". . . Put there by people such as yourself—in various countries—because I was fighting for my own version of freedom."

"Communism, undoubtedly!"

Moroka said softly, "I'm a South African, sir. Both my parents were killed in the 1960 riots. It seems that they had dark skins— even as you and I—and weren't able to see why that should keep them from freedom."

Fredric Ostrander spun back to Homer Crawford. "I'm not here to quibble with self-confessed malcontents. I've been sent to represent the State Department, to report to them, and, above all, to do what I can to prevent your activities from redounding to the further advantage of the Soviet Complex. I assume you can assign me quarters."

Straight-faced, Jack Peters translated this into Esperanto, and, straight-faced, Homer answered in the same language.

Jack turned back to the impatient C.I.A. man. "El Hassan welcomes the representative of the United States of the Americas and hopes this will be the first step toward diplomatic recognition between North Africa and your great country. He has instructed me to find you quarters, which, possibly you may have to share with delegations from Common Europe or"—Peters cleared his throat—"the Soviet Complex. He further suggests that it might be well, if you maintain communications with your superiors, to have sent to you books on Esperanto, the official language of North Africa."

Dave Moroka put in, "By the way, we'll have to go through your things. We can't allow any radio communication from El Hassan's camp, except through official El Hassan channels—for obvious military reasons."

Ostrander snorted, stared indignantly at Homer again, spun on his heel and stalked from the tent. Jack Peters followed him but not before tipping an uncharacteristic wink at Homer.

When they were gone, Homer sighed and looked at Dave Moroka. "That reminds me, how are our other delegations coming?"

The South African grinned ruefully. "They're playing it cool. Waiting to see what way to jump. Give El Hassan some real success, and they'll probably jump at the chance to be first to recognize him. Especially these Soviet Complex opportunists. They'd just love to suck you into their camp."

Isobel looked at him. "After that tearing down you gave poor Ostrander about the United States, now you rip into the Soviet Complex. Just where do you stand, Dave?"

Dave shrugged her question off, as though there were more important things. "I'm an El Hassan man," he said. "Let those two overgrown powers handle their own troubles."

Jimmy Peters spoke up for the first time since Ostrander entered the tent. "You know," he said, seriously, "I'm beginning to wonder if the world can afford nationalistic patriotism. Haven't we gone too far along the road to think of ourselves any longer as Americans, or Russians, or French, or West Indians, or whatever? Hasn't the human race grown up beyond that point?"

Kenny said mockingly, "What! Aren't you proud of being a West Indian, and a loyal subject of Her Majesty?"

Peters ignored his tone. "Why should I be proud of my country? It was an accident of birth with which I had nothing to do, that made me a West Indian, rather than a Canadian, a Chinese, a Norwegian, or whatever. Intelligently, I should be proud only of things that I, myself, have accomplished."

Bey said, "If we can stop waxing philosophic for a while and get back to how most efficiently to clobber these Arabs—"

The Hindu entered Kirill Menzhinsky's small office behind the Indian souvenir shop in the Tangier Zocco Chico and said, "The operative Anton is on the receiver."

The agent superior of the Chrez-vychainaya Komissiya for North Africa looked up from his desk and grunted acceptance of the message. He came to his feet and followed the other into a back room and took his place before a mouthpiece and screen.

The man whose party name was Anton nodded a greeting.

Kirill Menzhinsky said, "It's about time I heard from you, Anton."

"Yes. But the situation has been such that it was not easy to report."

"And now?"

"Briefly, I am at El Hassan's headquarters. You were correct. He is in actuality Homer Crawford. The others you mentioned are also with him, including the traitor Isobel Cunningham."

The Soviet Complex's agent allowed his eyebrows to rise.

Anton said flatly, "The dame has evidently renounced the party and now holds high rank in Crawford's inner circle."

"And you?"

"I am rapidly becoming his right-hand man. I am his press secretary and in charge of communications. Early in our acquaintanceship I was able to engineer an attempted assassination. I was able to, ah, save the life of El Hassan."

The Russian's eyes narrowed. "The assassins? Is there any chance that they might reveal your little trick?"

Anton grimaced. "I am not a fool, Kirill. Both of them were killed in the assassination attempt. El Hassan was most grateful."

"I see. And how would you sum up the present situation?"

"This area is swinging rapidly to El Hassan, but any sort of defeat and undoubtedly his followers would melt away. The bedouin are too volatile. Before he ever makes any real headway he will have to take the major commercial and industrial cities such as Dakar, Kano, Lagos, Accra, Freetown, Khartoum, and eventually, of course, Cairo, Casablanca, Algiers and so forth."

"And our friend El Hassan leans not at all in our direction?"

The man the Party called Anton shook his head. "He leans in no direction, except that which will unite and modernize North Africa. Neither do his immediate followers. They're a well-knit group and it seems unlikely that I could pry any of them away from him in case it became desirable."

"I see," Kirill Menzhinsky muttered. "I understand that a delegation from Moscow has arrived in El Hassan's camp. Have you contacted them?"

"Certainly not. My orders were to rise in the El Hassan hierarchy and await further orders. None of my current, ah, colleagues have any suggestion that I am identified with the Party. Which reminds me, an American C.I.A. man, Fredric Ostrander, has shown up. The fool seems to be under the impression that El Hassan is a Party tool."

"I know this Ostrander. Don't underestimate him, Anton.

He's an extremely competent operative in the clutch, as the Americans call it."

"Perhaps. But nevertheless, there is no indication that the El Hassan movement leans either to East or West, nor do I see any signs that it is apt to in the future."

The Russian was scowling. "I see. Then perhaps it will be necessary for us to do something to topple our El Hassan before he becomes much stronger, and to find another to unite North Africa."

Anton frowned in his turn. "I don't know. This man Crawford—and his followers, for that matter—are motivated by high ideals. As you have said, North Africa is not ready for our socioeconomic system. Men of the caliber of Homer Crawford could bring it into the modern age perhaps more quickly than another."

Menzhinsky chuckled. "Don't worry about it, Anton. Such matters of policy will be decided by others than you, or even me. Keep in touch with me more often, in the future, Anton."

"Yes, Comrade." His face faded from the screen.

Tamanrasset lies at an altitude of approximately 4,600 feet, about average for the Ahaggar plateau. Around it, such peaks as the Tahat reach 9,600 feet above sea level. The country is rugged, jagged, bleak beyond belief. With the possible exception of Southern Afghanistan in the Khyber area, there is no place in the world more suited for guerrilla warfare, less suited for the proper utilization of modern armor, particularly when the latter is forced to work without air cover.

Homer Crawford, equipped with an old-style telescope, was spread-eagled on top a rock outcropping, his only companion Isobel Cunningham. Directly before him, possibly two miles in distance, was the desert city of Tamanrasset, to the right, a kilometer or so, Amsel where palatable water was to be found at eighteen meters depth.

"Our friend, the colonel, is up to something," he grumbled.

She had a pair of binoculars, of considerably less power than his glass.

"It looks as though Guémama's boys are on the run," she said.

"As per orders. The primary theory of partisan warfare is not to get killed. The guerrilla never stands and fights. If the regular forces he opposes can bring him to bay, they've got him." He interrupted himself to clip out, "Look at that tank, darling! There on the left!"

Isobel tightened, looked at him quickly from the side of her eyes. No. He'd said it inadvertently, his mind concentrated on the fighting men below. She had often wondered where she stood with Homer Crawford the man, as opposed to El Hassan the idealist. The tip of her tongue licked the side of her mouth, as she surreptitiously took him in. But Crawford the man would have to wait, there was no time, no time.

Isobel swung her glasses. "The one starting to go in a circle? There, it stopped."

"One of the snipers got its commander," Homer said. "You can't fight a tank without the commander's head being up through the hatch. That's a popular fallacy. You can't see well enough to fight your tank unless you've got your head up. And that's suicide when you're against guerrillas. The colonel ought to send his infantry out first."

Isobel said, "What did you mean when you said that he's up to something?"

Homer's eye was still glued to the eyepiece of his glass. "He's leaving his entrenchments and sending his vehicles out to capture our . . . our strong points."

"You mean our water, don't you?"

Bey came snaking up to them on his belly. He came abreast of Homer and brought forth his own binoculars. He watched for a moment and then muttered a curse under his breath.

"Guémama better start pulling back those men more quickly," he said.

"He will. He's a good man," Homer told him. "What's up?"

"Evidently, Colonel Ibrahim has decided to come out of retirement. He's sent small motorized elements to Effok, In Fedjeg, Otoul and even to Tahifet."

"And—?"

"And has taken them all, of course. Our men fall back, fighting a stubborn rear-guard action, taking as few casualties as possible."

"I don't get it," Homer bit out. "He's using up his fuel and ammunition and losing more men than we are. Certainly he can't figure, with the thousand odd troops he has, to be able to take and hold enough of the oases and water holes in this vicinity to push us out completely."

Bey said, "What worries me is the possibility that he knows something we don't. That he's figuring on being relieved or has a new source of fuel, ammunition and men on tap."

"The roads are cut. Our men hold every source of water from here to Libya and the Reunited Nations has put thumbs down on aircraft which eliminates an air lift."

"Yeah," Bey said, unhappily.

That evening, following the day's last meal, Cliff came into the headquarters tent grinning, broadly. "Hey, guess what we've liberated."

"A bottle of Scotch?" Kenny said hopefully.

"A king-size portable radio transmitter. Ralph Sandell knew about it. The Sahara Afforestation Project people were going to use it to propagandize the tribesmen into coming in and taking jobs in the new oases."

Dave Moroka, who'd been censoring press releases, shook his head. "That's why we need an El Hassan in this country," he complained. "They put a couple of million dollars into a radio transmitter, never asking themselves how many of the bedouin own radios."

Jack Peters said, "Wait a moment, you chaps. Didn't Bey capture a couple of Arab Legion radio technicians today?"

"They defected to us," Homer Crawford said, looking up from an improvised desk where he was poring over some supply papers with Isobel. "What did you have in mind, Jack?"

"There are radios in Tamanrasset. In fact, there's probably a radio in every one of those military vehicles of Ibrahim's. Why can't we blanket these Arab Union chaps with El Hassan propaganda? Quite a few of them are from Libya, Tunisia and Egypt. In short, they're Africans and susceptible to El Hassan's dream."

"Good man. Take over the details, Jack," Homer said. He went back to his work with Isobel.

Jimmy Peters entered with some papers in hand. He said, seriously, "The temperature is rising in the Reunited Nations—and everywhere else, for that matter. Damascus and Cairo have been getting increasingly belligerent. Homer, it looks as though the Arab Union is getting ready to go out on a limb. Weeks have passed since Colonel Ibrahim first took Tamanrasset and the Reunited Nations, the United States, the Soviet Complex and all others interested in North Africa, have failed to do anything.

Everybody, evidently, afraid of precipitating something that couldn't be ended."

All eyes went to Homer Crawford who ran a black hand back over his hair in weariness. "I know," he said. "Something is about to blow. Dave has sent some of his best men into Tamanrasset to pick up gossip in the souks. Morale was dragging bottom among the legionnaires just a couple of days ago. Now they seem to have a new lease."

"In spite of the sabotage our people have been committing?" Isobel said.

"That's falling off somewhat," Cliff said. "At first our more enthusiastic followers were able to pull everything from heaving Molotov Cocktails into tanks, to pouring sugar in hover-jeep gas tanks, but the legionnaires have both smartened up and gotten very tough."

"Good," Dave Moroka said now.

They looked at him.

"Atrocities," he said. "In order to guard against sabotage, the legionnaires will be taking measures that will antagonize the people in Tamanrasset. They'll shoot a couple of teenage kids, or something, then they'll have a city-wide mess on their hands."

Isobel said unhappily, "It seems a nasty way to win a war."

Dave grunted his contempt of her opinion. "There is no way of winning a war other than a nasty one."

Bey came in, yawning hugely. His energy was inconceivable to the others. So far as was known, he hadn't slept, other than sitting erect in a moving vehicle, for the past four days. He said to Homer, "Fred Ostrander has been bending my ear for the past hour or so. Do you want to talk to him?"

"About what?" Homer said.

"I don't know. He has a lot of questions. I think he's beginning to suspect—just suspect, understand—that possibly the whole bunch of us aren't receiving our daily instructions from either Moscow or Peking."

Dave and Cliff both laughed.

Homer sighed and said, "Show him in. He's the only thing we have in the way of a contact with the United States of the Americas and sooner or later we're going to have to make our peace with both them and the Soviet Complex. In fact, what we're probably going to have to do is play one against the other, getting grants, loans, economic assistance—"

"Technicians, teachers, arms," Bey continued the list.

Kenny Ballalou looked at him and snorted. "Arms! If there's anything this part of the world doesn't need it's more arms. In fact, that goes for the rest of the world, too. In the old days when the great nations were first beginning to attempt to line up the neutrals they sent aid to such countries by the billions—and most of it in arms. How ridiculous can you get? Putting arms in the hands of most of the governments of that time was like handing a loaded pistol to an idiot."

Bey hung his head in mock humility. "I bow before your wisdom," he said. He left the room to get Ostrander.

The C.I.A. man had lost a fraction of his belligerence, but none of his arrogance and natty appearance. Homer wondered vaguely how the other managed to remain so spruce in the inadequate desert camp.

Jack Peters said, "What did you wish to ask El Hassan? I will translate."

"Never mind that, Jack," Homer said. "We'll get tougher about using our official language when we've gone a little further in building our new government." He said to Ostrander, "What can I do for you? Obviously, my time, is limited."

Fredric Ostrander said, "I've been gathering material for reports to my superiors. I've been doing a good deal of questioning, and, frankly, even prying around."

Cliff grunted.

Ostrander went on. "I've also read the various press releases, manifestoes and so forth that your assistants have been compiling."

"We know," Homer said. "We haven't put any obstacles in your way. We haven't any particular secrets, Mr. Ostrander."

"You disguise the fact that you are an American," the C.I.A. man said accusingly.

Homer said slowly, "Only because El Hassan is not an American, Mr. Ostrander. He is an African with African solutions to African problems. That is what he must be if he is to accomplish his task."

Ostrander seemed to switch subjects. "See here, Crawford, the State Department is not completely opposed to the goal of uniting North Africa. It would solve many problems, both African and international."

Kenny Ballalou laughed softly. "You mean, you're on our side?"

Ostrander turned to him, for once not incensed at being needled. "Possibly more than you'd think," he rapped. He turned back again to Homer Crawford. "The question becomes, why do you think that you are the man for the job? Who gave you the go-ahead?"

Bey, who had settled down into a folding camp chair, now came to his feet, his tired face angry.

But Homer waved him to silence. "Hold it," he said. Then to Ostrander. "It doesn't work that way. It's not something you decide to do because you're thirsty for power, or greedy for money. You're pushed into it. Do you think Washington, a retired Virginian planter wrapped up in his estate and his family, wanted to spend years leading the revolutionary armies through the wilderness that was America in those days? He was thrust into the job, there was no one else more competent to take it. Men make the times, Ostrander, but the times also make the men. Look at Lenin and Trotsky. Three months before the October Revolution, Lenin wrote that he never expected to see in his lifetime the Bolsheviks come to power. Within those months he was at the head of government and Trotsky, a former bookworm who had never fired a gun in his life, was head of the Red Army and being proclaimed a military genius."

Ostrander was scowling at him, but his face was thoughtful.

Homer said quietly, "It's not always an easy thing, to have power thrust into your hands. Not always a desirable thing." His voice went quieter still. "Only a short time ago it led me to the necessity of . . . killing . . . my best friend."

"And mine," Isobel said softly, almost under her breath.

Dave Moroka said, "Abe Baker," before he caught himself.

Kenny Ballalou looked at him strangely. "Did you know Abe?"

The South African recovered. "I've heard several of you mention him from time to time. He was a commie, wasn't he?"

"Yes," Homer said without inflection. "And a man. He saved my life on more than one occasion. As long as we worked together with only Africa in mind, there was no conflict. But Abe had a further, and, to him, greater alliance."

He turned his attention back to the C.I.A. man. "A man does

what he must do," he finished simply. "I did not ask to become El Hassan."

Ostrander said, "Your motivation is possibly beside the point. The thing is that the battle for men's minds continues and your program, eventually, must align with the West."

"And get clobbered in the stampeding around between the two great powers," Kenny said dryly.

"You've got to take your stand," Ostrander said. "I'd rather die under the neutron bomb, than spend the rest of my life on my knees under a Soviet Complex government. Wouldn't you?" His eyes went from one of them to the other, defiantly.

Homer said slowly. "No, even though that was the only alternative, which is unlikely. Not if it meant finishing off the whole human race at the same time." He shook his head. "If it were only me, it might be different. But if it was a matter of nuclear war the whole race might well end. Given such circumstances, I'd be proud to remain on my knees the rest of my life. You see, Ostrander, you make the mistake of thinking the Soviet socio-economic system is a permanent thing. It isn't. It's changing daily, even as our own socio-economic system is. Even if the Soviet Complex were to dominate the whole world, it would be but a temporary phase in man's history. Their regime, in its time, right or wrong, will go under in man's march to whatever his destiny might be. Some day it will be only a memory, and so will the socio-economic systems of the West. No institutions are less permanent than politico-economic ones."

"I don't agree with you," Ostrander snapped.

"Obviously," Homer shrugged. "However, this is another problem. El Hassan deals with North Africa. The other problems you bring up we admit, but at this stage are not dealing with them. Our dream is in Africa. Perhaps the Africans will be forced to taking other stands, to dreaming new dreams, twenty or thirty years from now. When that time comes, I assume the new problems will be faced. By that time there will probably be no need for El Hassan."

Ostrander looked at him and bit his lip in thought.

It came to him now that he had never won in his contests with Homer Crawford, and that he would probably never win. No matter how strong his convictions, in the presence of the other man, something went out of him. There was strength in Crawford that must be experienced to be understood. When he talked, he held you, and your own opinions became nothing—stupidities on your lips. He had a dream, and in conversation with him, all other things dropped away and nothing was of importance but that dream. A dream? Possibly disease was the better word. And so highly contagious.

While they talked, an aide had entered and handed a report to Bey-ag-Akhamouk. He read it and closed his eyes in weariness.

"What's up, Bey," Homer asked.

"I don't know. Colonel Ibrahim has stepped up his attacks in all directions. At least two thirds of his force is on the offensive. It doesn't make much sense. But it must make sense to him, or he wouldn't be doing it."

Ostrander said, and to everyone's surprise there seemed to be an element of worry in his voice too, "I know Colonel Midan Ibrahim, met him in Cairo and in Baghdad on various occasions. He's considered one of the best men in the Arab Legion. He doesn't make military blunders."

Bey said, "Come on, Kenny. Let's round up Guémama and take a look at the front." He led the way from the tent.

There was a guard posted before the tent which doubled as press and communications center, and the private quarters of David Moroka.

The figure that approached timidly was garbed in the traditional clothing of the young women of the Tégéhé Mellet tribe of the Tuareg and bore an imzad in her left hand, while her right held a corner of her gandoura over her face.

The guard, of the Kel Rela tribe, eyed the one-stringed violin with its string of hair and sounding box made of half a gourd covered with a thin membrane of skin, and grinned. A Tuareg maid was accustomed to sing and to make the high whining tones of desert music on the imzad before submitting to her lover's embrace. Wallahi! but these women of the Tégéhé Mellet were shameless.

"Where do you go?" he said gruffly. "El Hassan's vizier has ordered that he is occupied and none should approach."

"He awaits me," she wavered. There was kohl about her eyes, and indigo at the corners of her mouth.

"We met at the tendi last night and he bid me come to his tent. It is for me he waits."

Wallahi! but his leader had taste, the sentry decided.

"Pass," he said gruffly. Even a vizier of such importance as this one must need solace at times, he decided philosophically.

She slipped past silently to the tent entrance where the Tuareg guard noticed she paused for a long moment before entering. He grinned into his tagelmoust. Aiii, the little bird was timid before the hawk.

She stood for a moment listening, and then slipped inside, dropping the desert musical instrument to the ground. Dave Moroka's back was to her and even as she entered he flicked off the switch of the video-radio into which he had been speaking and scowled at it.

When he stood and began to turn, she covered him with the small pocket pistol. She had an ease in handling it which denoted competence.

His eyebrows went up, but he remained silent, waiting for her gambit.

Isobel said evenly, "You're a Party member, aren't you, Dave?"

"Why do you say that?"

She nodded infinitesimally to the set. "You were reporting just now. I heard enough just as I came in."

He took in her disguise. "My guard isn't as efficient as I had thought," Dave said wryly.

Isobel said, "You knew Abe Baker, didn't you?"

He looked at her, expressionlessly.

She said, "I already knew you belonged to the Party, Dave. No matter how competent an agent, it's something difficult to hide from any other long-time member. There's a terminology you use—such as calling it the Soviet Union, rather than Russia. No commie ever says Russia, it's always the Soviet Union. You can tell, just as a Roman Catholic can tell a person raised in the Church, even though the other has dropped away, or even as one Jew can tell another. Yes, I've known you were a Party member for some time, Dave."

"And?" the South African said.

"Why are you here?"

Dave Moroka said, "For the same reason you are, to further the El Hassan dream, the uniting and modernization of the continent of my racial heritage."

"But you are still a Party member and still report to your superiors."

Dave Moroka looked at the tiny gun she held in her hand.

"Don't try it," she said. "I have seen you in action, Dave. I have never seen a man move so ruthlessly fast . . . but don't try it."

"No reason to," he bit out. "Come on, let's go see Homer."

She was slightly taken aback, but not enough to release her control for even a split second. "Lead the way," she said.

Even at this time of evening, the headquarters tent was brightly lit and most of the immediate El Hassan staff still at work. Homer Crawford looked up as they entered.

Cliff Jackson saw the gun first and said, "Holy Mackerel, Isobel."

Fredric Ostrander was sitting to one side in discussion with the sober faced Jack Peters. He took in the gun and slowly came to his feet, obviously expecting climax.

Isobel said, "Dave's taking over control of communications had method. I just found him reporting to what must have been a superior . . . in the Party."

Homer Crawford looked from the South African to Isobel, then back to Dave again, without speaking. His eyes were questioning.

Dave said, his voice sharp. "I haven't time for details now. Isobel's right. I was a Party member."

"Was?" Ostrander chuckled. "That's the understatement of the year. I hadn't got around to revealing the fact as yet, but our friend Dave is the notorious Anton, one of the Soviet Complex's most competent hatchetmen."

Dave looked at him only briefly. "Was," he reiterated. He turned his attention to Homer and to Bey, who was staring tired dismay at this new addition to the load.

Homer still held his peace, waiting for the other to go on.

"I found out tonight why Colonel Ibrahim is attacking, instead of pulling in his horns as reason would dictate." Dave paused for emphasis. "The Soviet Complex has thrown its weight, in this matter at least, on the side of the Arab Union. They have insisted that Sven Zetterberg be dismissed as head of the Sahara Division of the African Development Project and that his threat to use Reunited Nations aircraft if the local fighting spreads to the air, be repudiated."

Kenny blurted, "Good grief . . . that means—"

Dave looked around at them, one by one. "It means," he said, "that the Arab Legion is going to be reinforced tomorrow morning by a full regiment of paratroopers."

"Holy Mackerel," Cliff groaned. "We've had it. Another regiment of crack troops in Tamanrasset and we'll never take the town."

Dave shook his head. "That's not the big thing. The paratroopers aren't going to drop in Tamanrasset. They're going to hit every oasis, every water hole, in a circumference of two hundred miles."

There was an empty silence.

Homer Crawford said finally, evenly, "In the expectation that every follower of El Hassan in the Sahara will either surrender or die of thirst, eh?" He didn't seem sufficiently impressed by the threatening disaster. He looked at Dave questioningly. "Why do you bother to tell us, Dave, if you're on the other side?"

Dave grunted sour amusement. "Because I've just become a full member of the team. I resigned from the Party tonight."

"Brother," Bey said, "you sure pick a helluva time to join up." He obviously was expressing the opinions of the majority.

Homer Crawford came to his feet and looked around at them. "All right," he said. "A new complication. Let's face up to it. There's always an answer. We're in the clutch, let's fight our way out."

Largely, they stared at him, but he ignored their dismay. He looked from one to the other. "We need some ideas. Let's kick it around. Isobel, Cliff, Jack, Kenny—?" His eyes went from one to the other. Obviously his own mind was churning.

They shook their heads dumbly.

Kenny said, "Ideas! We've had it, Homer!"

Homer Crawford spun on him and now the force they all knew was emanating from him. He laughed his scorn. "A month ago we were half a dozen fugitives. Now we're an army besieging a city. And you say we've had it? Listen, Kenny, if we have to we'll go back to being half a dozen fugitives again—those of us that are left. But the dream goes on! However, we're not going to have to. We're too near victory in this stage of the operation to sit down on the job because of a threatened reverse. Now then, let's kick. it around. Jimmy! Dave! Kenny! Ostrander!"

Fredric Ostrander raised his eyebrows only slightly at being included in their number.

Bey, for once, was seemingly too exhausted to be brought to new enthusiasm. He tossed a detail map of Tamanrasset to the table. "And I'd just worked out a bang-up scheme for infiltrating into town, joining up with our adherents there, and seizing it while most of Ibrahim's men were out in the desert, trying to capture our nearer water holes."

Homer snapped, "It sounds like it still might have possibilities."

Ostrander looked down at the map, his face very tight. "How long would it take?"

Bey scowled at him, defeat dulling his mind. "What?"

"How long do you figure it would take to infiltrate Tamanrasset and capture it? Behind Ibrahim's back, so to speak."

Bey grunted. "A couple of hours in the early morning. I had a beautiful picture of the colonel's armor out in the desert, cut off from its petroleum supplies and ammunition dump while we held the town. Some of our men, the former veterans of the French West African forces, could have even operated the antitank guns he has mounted at Fort Laperrine."

The C.I.A. man's mouth worked.

Homer Crawford's eyes pierced him.

Ostrander walked over to the radio before which Kenny Ballalou sat. "See if you can raise Colonel Ibrahim for me."

Kenny scowled at him. "Why?"

"Do it."

Kenny looked at Homer Crawford.

Homer said, "O.K. Do it."

Kenny shrugged and turned to the set. While the others watched, Crawford's face alert, his eyes narrowed, the rest of them dull in apathy, the face of Colonel Ibrahim finally faded in on the screen.

Fredric Ostrander took his place at the instrument. He nodded, formally. "Greetings, Colonel, it seems a long time since last we met in Amman."

The Arab Legion officer smiled politely. "I had heard that you represented the State Department in this area, Mr. Ostrander, and have been somewhat surprised that you failed to make Tamanrasset your headquarters. It would have been pleasant to have renewed old friendship."

Ostrander cleared his throat. "I am afraid that would have been difficult, Colonel, particularly in view of the stand of my government at this time."

On the screen, the other's eyebrows went up.

Ostrander said evenly, "Colonel, we have just been informed that a regiment of paratroopers has been put at your disposal and that they plan to land at various points in the Sahara in the morning."

The colonel said stiffly, "This is military information which I am not free to discuss, Mr. Ostrander."

Frederic Ostrander went on, his voice still even. "We have further been informed that the Reunited Nations has withdrawn its ban on aircraft, which would seem to free your paratroop carrying planes."

The colonel remained silent, waiting for the bombshell. It was obvious that he expected a bombshell.

Ostrander said, "As representative of the State Department I warn you that if these paratroop carrying planes take off tomorrow morning, the Seventh Airfleet of the United States of the Americas will enter the conflict on the side of El Hassan. Good evening, Colonel."

The C.I.A. man reached out and flicked the switch that killed the set. Then he took the snowy white handkerchief from the breast pocket of his jacket and wiped his mouth.

Isobel said, "Heavens to Betsy."

Kenny said indignantly, "Good grief, you fool, it won't take more than hours for your superiors to repudiate you. Then what happens?"

"By then, I assume, the battle will be over and Tamanrasset in El Hassan's hands. The Arab Union will then think twice before committing their paratroopers, particularly with captured armor in El Hassan's hands."

"And your name will be mud," Kenny blurted.

Ostrander looked at Homer Crawford. "Gentlemen, you must remember that I, too, am an African. I had thought that perhaps there would be a position for me on El Hassan's staff."

Crawford reached for the Tommy-Noiseless that leaned up against the improvised desk at which he worked. He said, "Let's get moving, Bey. We haven't much time. We're going to have to be able to announce its capture from Tamanrasset in a couple of hours."

"Not you," Bey said, grabbing up his own weapon and motioning with his head for Kenny and Cliff to come along. "You're El Hassan and can't be risked."

"I'm coming," Homer said flatly. "It's about time El Hassan began taking some of the same risks his followers seem to be willing to face. Besides, the men will fight better with me out in front. Got a gun, Fred?"

Ostrander said, "No. Where am I issued one?"

"I'll show you," Homer said, stuffing extra clips in his bush jacket pockets. "Come on, Dave."

The whole group began heading for the open air, Bey already yelling orders.

Fredric Ostrander looked at Dave Moroka. "Strange bedfellows," he said.

Moroka grinned wryly. "My long view hasn't changed," he said. "It's just that this African matter takes precedence right now."

"Nor mine, of course," Ostrander said. He cleared his throat. "However, I hope you last out the night. El Hassan needs strong men."

"Same to you," Moroka said gruffly. "Let's get going, or the fight will be over while we hand each other flowers."

EPILOGUE

El Hassan stood in the smoking, war-wasted ruin of Fort Laperine, his mind empty. The body of Jack Peters was ten feet to his left, burned beyond recognition and crumpled over a flame thrower which he'd eliminated in the last few moments of the fighting. Had he let his eyes go out the gun port before which he stood, it might have been possible for El Hassan to have picked out the bodies of David Moroka and Fredric Ostrander amidst those of the several hundred Haratin serfs who had swarmed out of the souk area at the crucial moment and stormed the half manned fort—unarmed save for knives and farm implements.

To his right, Dr. Warren Harding Smythe supervised two Tuareg who were carrying off the broken body of Kenny Ballalou; there was still faint life in it.

The doctor looked at him. "You are satisfied, I assume?"

El Hassan failed to hear him.

Smythe turned and stomped off, following his impressed nurses.

In the distance, Bey-ag-Akhamouk called hoarse orders from an over-strained throat, placing guns for a counterattack that would never come. The Arab Legion was broken and Colonel Ibrahim a prisoner. Large numbers of the survivors were defecting to the banner of El Hassan.

He threw his empty Tommy-Noiseless to the side. All he wanted now was sleep, the surcease of a few hours of oblivion.

Isobel, her face wan from the horror of the agony of the combat whose result was everywhere visible, was picking her way through the wreckage with Cliff Jackson.

El Hassan looked at her absently. Whatever message she bore held little interest to him.

Cliff said, "India has recognized El Hassan as legal head of state of all North Africa. It is expected that Australia will follow before the week is out."

El Hassan nodded. For the time, not caring.

Isobel said, "We have other word. It came by messenger." She closed her eyes in pain and handed him a small box.

He opened it and recognized the ring on the enclosed finger. He looked up at them.

Cliff Jackson growled low in his throat. "Elmer Allen. He's

been captured by a leader of the Ouled Touameur clan of the Ouled Allouch tribe. You know this Abd-el-Kader?"

El Hassan was staring down at the finger, his mind slowly clearing of its fatigue. "He belongs to the Berazga division of the Chaambra confederation. I had a run-in with him a few months ago and had him jailed. He's nothing but a desert bandit on the make."

Cliff said, "He's escaped, has thrown his weight behind the Arab Union, proclaimed himself the Madhi and is uniting Algeria and parts of Morocco and Tunisia like a wildfire. The marabouts and Shorfa are backing him."

"Proclaimed himself the Mahdi?" Isobel said in question.

El Hassan turned to the girl and took a deep breath. "The original Mahdi was the holiest prophet since Mohammed and according to the more superstitious Moslems, he's still alive. According to Islamic tradition, he periodically shows up again in the desert and makes various predictions. When he does, it almost always winds up with a jedah, a holy war. Don't you remember in history the anti-British Mahdi at Khartoum, the killing of Chinese Gordon and so forth? That Mahdi was the son of a Dongola carpenter and he managed to conquer two million square miles in two years."

"But, what has this got to do with this Abd-el-Kader?"

"He's evidently proclaimed himself sort of a reincarnation of the original Mahdi. He's out to do the same thing we are—to unite North Africa. But in his case he doesn't exactly have the same dream and he's working under the green ensign of the Pan-Islamic Arab Union."

"And has Elmer Allen captive."

"Yes, he has Elmer." El Hassan's tone of voice turned sharp. "Cliff, go get Bey. Tell him we're forming a flying column and heading north."

Cliff was gone. El Hassan turned back to the girl. "You know, Isobel," he said softly, slowly, "in history there is no happy ending, ever. There is no ending at all. It goes from one crisis to another, but there is no ending."